U0073642

哈福

哈福

1億人都在用的英語書

大人、小孩的 10分鐘會話速成課

張瑪麗◎著

哈福

[前言]

英文再好，也要說得出口才算數

笨蛋！英語不是用背的，那是蠢人；反覆閱讀，才是聰明的。你只要把一本英文書，反覆看 10 遍，純熟掌握，說起英文，就會很道地。英語啞巴，也能變身英語達人！

每天不用多，10 分鐘就夠了，10 分鐘是一個人最大的專注力。10 分鐘就可以讓你的英語起死回生。

有錢人玩得的是與金錢的生死時速。學英語的人想的是與英語的生死時速。

俄羅斯有個 4 歲女孩，會說 7 國語言：英語、法語、德語、俄語、中文、西班牙語、阿拉伯語，像這樣的語言天才，絕對不是用背就會的，要熟練、掌握，沒有語言恐懼症，才能練就會說 7 國語言的小天才。

你發現在這個時代，走在街頭「撞」上外國人的機率 very high ？

你家的超級小寶貝，英語越來越厲害，動不動就喜歡拿英語跟你「嗆聲」，你心裡想，好歹我學生時代，英文也曾經「不小心」考過 100 ！

求職面試，薪水不怎麼高，英語能力卻要求百分百？ Oh!

my God! 我的英文其實很厲害，但卻怎麼用力也講不出來！

不要錯過，學語言的黃金塑造期

從小到大，我們在學校所學的是英語的「知識」，而非英語的「說法」，強調讀與寫，忽略聽與說，一旦過了學語言的黃金塑造期後，想要突破膽量，開口說英語，卻礙於語言的思考已固著於文法結構，因此才無法順暢、輕鬆地用簡單的口語表達出來。

本書內容皆為日常生活中的生活對話，不管面臨結交外國朋友，或是出國旅行都相當實用，讓你不再是英語啞巴！

為了克服你學習語言的障礙，建議你從生活中的口語開始！以下有幾個絕對能夠讓你 Fun 輕鬆說英語的招數。

★如果你一說英語就容易手腳發軟，那就 ....

Forget it! 先看一場電影再說吧。

★如果你一想到說得不好就覺得很丟臉，那就 ....

降低一點「智商」，讓自己像個小孩，有時不妨也裝裝可愛。

★如果你老是覺得舌頭僵硬、嘴巴長繭，那就 ....

做做「嘴舌暖身」運動。ㄟ ...... 這個就看個人的喜好囉！例如，嚼嚼口香糖之類的嘛！

★如果你覺得實在忍不住想秀一口流利的英語，那麼，本書絕對可以幫你達成心願。

1000 句生活會話實用例句，搭配專業標準發音 MP3，相信你的舌頭不會再打結，你的腦袋沒有時間空白，你的嘴巴沒有機會停下來。

★如果你覺得這樣還不夠，建議你可以放膽的站在大街上，仔細掃瞄、對準目標，看看哪個幸運兒是你中意的練習對象喔！

本系列特色

- 100%原汁原味－特聘專業英語教材專家撰寫，內容自然生活化。
- 句型簡單易說－新鮮流行的休閒話題，隨時隨地朗朗上口，不當機。
- 錄音嚴謹專業－由美籍專業播音員精心錄製的標準發音 MP3，腔調自然純正。
- 標準口語速度－另外有以一般外藉人士說話的速度，搭配實境音效與配樂錄製之 MP3，學習起來絕對輕鬆不打盹。

Contents

Contents

CHAPTER 3 AT THE SCHOOL 學校生活

CHAPTER 4 Vacation 度假、休假

Contents

CHAPTER 5 SOCIAL ACTIVITY 社交活動

CHAPTER 6 HOBBY/SPORTS 嗜好和運動

CHAPTER 7 RESERVATION 預訂

CHAPTER 8 COMPLAINING 抱怨

本書使用方法

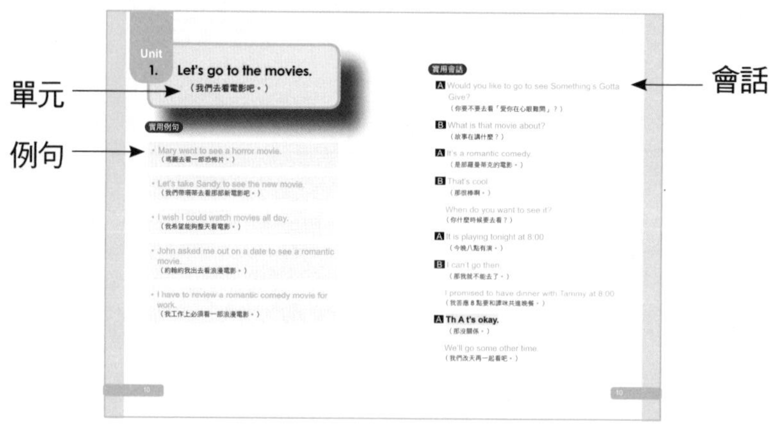

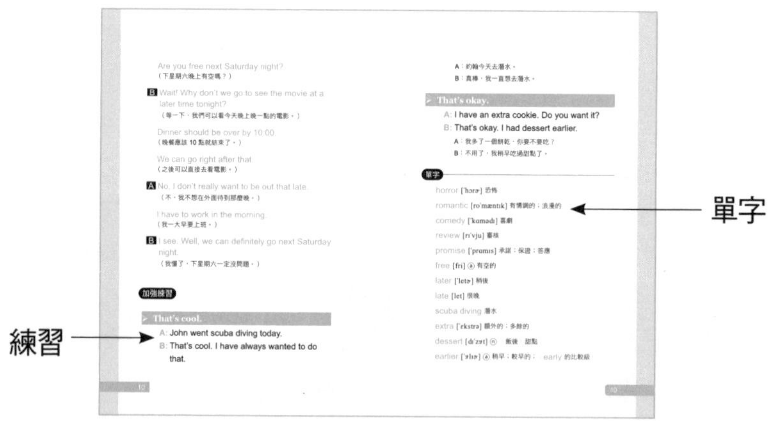

CHAPTER 1

MOVIES

電影

Unit 1. Let's go to the movies.

（我們去看電影吧。）

實用例句

- Mary went to see a horror movie.
（瑪麗去看一部恐怖片。）

- Let's take Sandy to see the new movie.
（我們帶珊蒂去看那部新電影吧。）

- I wish I could watch movies all day.
（我希望能夠整天看電影。）

- John asked me out on a date to see a romantic movie.
（約翰約我出去看浪漫電影。）

- I have to review a romantic comedy movie for work.
（我工作上必須看一部浪漫電影。）

實用會話

A Would you like to go to see Something's Gotta Give?
（你要不要去看「愛你在心眼難開」？）

B What is that movie about?
（故事在講什麼？）

A It's a romantic comedy.
（是部羅曼蒂克的電影。）

B That's cool.
（那很棒啊。）

When do you want to see it?
（你什麼時候要去看？）

A It is playing tonight at 8:00.
（今晚八點有演。）

B I can't go then.
（那我就不能去了。）

I promised to have dinner with Tammy at 8:00.
（我答應 8 點要和譚咪共進晚餐。）

A **That's okay.**
（那沒關係。）

We'll go some other time.
（我們改天再一起看吧。）

Are you free next Saturday night?
（下星期六晚上有空嗎？）

B Wait! Why don't we go to see the movie at a later time tonight?
（等一下，我們可以看今天晚上晚一點的電影。）

Dinner should be over by 10:00.
（晚餐應該 10 點就結束了。）

We can go right after that.
（之後可以直接去看電影。）

A No, I don't really want to be out that late.
（不，我不想在外面待到那麼晚。）

I have to work in the morning.
（我一大早要上班。）

B I see. Well, we can definitely go next Saturday night.
（我懂了，下星期六一定沒問題。）

加強練習

➢ That's cool.

A: John went scuba diving today.

B: That's cool. I have always wanted to do that.

A：約翰今天去潛水。

B：真棒，我一直想去潛水。

➢ That's okay.

A: I have an extra cookie. Do you want it?

B: That's okay. I had dessert earlier.

A：我多了一個餅乾，你要不要吃？

B：不用了，我稍早吃過甜點了。

單字

horror ['hɔrɚ] 恐怖

romantic [ro'mæntɪk] 有情調的；浪漫的

comedy ['kɑmədɪ] 喜劇

review [rɪ'vju] 審核

promise ['prɑmɪs] 承諾；保證；答應

free [fri] ⓐ 有空的

later ['letɚ] 稍後

late [let] 很晚

scuba diving 潛水

extra ['ɛkstrə] 額外的；多餘的

dessert [dɪ'zɝt] ⓝ（飯後）甜點

earlier ['ɝlɪɚ] ⓐ 稍早；較早的；（early 的比較級）

Unit 2.

What time does the movie start?

（電影什麼時候開始？）

實用例句

- Would you like to purchase the movie tickets in advance?
  （你想要預購電影票嗎？）

- I hate the long ticket lines at the movies.
  （我討厭在電影院大排長龍。）

- Did you bring your student I.D. card to get the student discount?
  （你有帶學生證嗎？這樣才可以享有折扣。）

- How many tickets did you want to purchase for the movie?
  （你想買幾張電影票？）

- Could you buy my movie ticket? I will pay you back later.
  （你可以先幫我買票嗎？我稍後再給你錢。）

實用會話

A Should I buy our movie tickets online or at the theatre?
（我應該用網路購票？還是在電影院現場買票？）

B What time does the movie start?
（電影什麼時候開始？）

A It will begin playing in one hour.
（一小時候開始。）

B I think we have enough time to go to the theatre to buy them.
（我想我們有足夠的時間到電影院再買票。）

A But this is opening weekend.
（但這週是首映。）

The lines may be really long.
（隊伍可能會排很長。）

B **That's true**.
（那倒也是。）

Maybe you should go to the theatre's website and buy them.
（也許你應該去電影院的網站購票。）

A Ok. I think that is a good idea.
（好啊，我想這是個不錯的主意。）

Could I use your laptop?
（我能用你的手提電腦嗎？）

B **Sure**. I will get it from my office.
（當然，我去把它從辦公室拿出來。）

Do you need the theatre's web address?
（你需要電影院的網址嗎？）

A No, I have it.
（不用，我知道網址。）

I am glad that we don't have to wait in line at the theatre anymore.
（好高興不用去電影院排隊等候了。）

B Me, too. We can wait in line to buy popcorn instead.
（我有同感，我們可以去排隊買爆玉米花。）

加強練習

➢ That's true.

A: We should all get a good night's sleep on Friday.

B: That's true. We have to be up at 6:00am on Saturday for basketball practice.

A：我們大家星期五晚上應該都要睡個好覺。

B：那到也是，因為星期六早上 6 點就要起床去練習籃球了。

➢ Sure.

A: Could you help me with my math homework?

B: Sure. Why don't we go over it tomorrow afternoon?

A：你可以幫忙我的數學作業嗎？

B：當然，我們明天下午一起做數學作業吧。

單字

purchase [ˈpɝtʃəs] 購買

advance [ədˈvæns] ⓝ 預先

line [laɪn] 排隊

ticket [ˈtɪkɪt] 票

theatre [ˈθɪətɚ] 戲院

Unit

3. At the concession stand

（點心櫃檯）

實用例句

- Do you want butter and salt on your popcorn?
  （你的爆米花上要不要加奶油和鹽？）

- (To the cashier) I would like two hot dogs and two small popcorns, please.
  （對櫃員說：我想要兩隻熱狗和兩個小的爆玉米花。）

- (cashier talking to the customer) Your total is $4.15.
  （櫃員回答說：總共是 4 元 15 分。）

- I am so hungry; I can't wait to get my nachos and candy.
  （我好餓了，等不及要吃玉米捲餅和糖果了。）

- What kind of drink would you like?
  （你想要喝什麼飲料？）

實用會話

A I need to go to the concession stand.
（我需要去點心櫃檯一趟。）

Want me to bring you something?
（你要不要買些什麼？）

B I don't know. What do they have?
（我不知道耶。他們賣些什麼呢？）

A They have hot dogs and nachos.
（他們有熱狗和玉米捲餅。）

B Do they have cheese sticks?
（他們有賣起士棒嗎？）

A I am not sure.
（我不確定。）

I can ask the person at the counter when I get to the concession stand.
（我可以去問問櫃檯的人。）

B **Ok, great.**
（那很不錯啊。）

If they don't have them, please get me a box of candy.
（如果沒賣的話，就幫我買一盒糖果吧。）

A What kind?
（什麼樣的糖果？）

B I want a box of peanut M&M's.
（我想要一盒花生 MM 巧克力。）

I love eating those while at the movies.
（我喜歡看電影時吃那些糖果。）

A **Cool**. Well, I'll be back in a bit.
（聽起來很不錯，我馬上就回來。）

B Thanks a lot.
（多謝啦。）

加強練習

➢ Ok, great.

A: I finished cleaning the bathroom.
B: Ok, great. **Now,** please wash the dishes.

A：我打掃完浴室了。
B：太好了，現在去洗碗吧。

➢ Cool.

A: Today, I went to the museum of art.
B: Cool. Did you like the paintings and sculptures?

A：我今天去了美術博物館。

B：太棒了，你喜歡畫作和雕刻品嗎？

單字

popcorn [ˈpɑpˈkɔrn] 爆玉米花

candy [ˈkændɪ] 糖果

hungry [ˈhʌŋgrɪ] 餓

customer [ˈkʌstəmɚ] ⓝ 顧客

drink [drɪŋk] ⓥ 喝（飲料）；ⓝ 飲料

concession [kənˈsɛʃən]

stand [stænd] 小攤子

counter [ˈkaʊntɚ] 櫃檯

finish [ˈfɪnɪʃ] 完成

painting [ˈpentɪŋ] 圖畫

sculpture [ˈskʌlptʃɚ] 雕刻

museum [mjuˈzɪəm] 博物館

Unit 4. What kind of movies do you like?

（你喜歡什麼樣的電影？）

實用例句

- Do you like scary movies?
  （你喜歡恐怖電影嗎？）

- Does Jimmy like comedies?
  （吉米喜歡喜劇嗎？）

- What movie would you like to see this weekend?
  （你這個週末想看什麼電影？）

- Do you know if John liked The Lord of the Rings?
  （你知道約翰會不會喜歡看「魔戒」？）

- I like watching mystery movies.
  （我喜歡看懸疑片。）

實用會話

A What kind of movies do you prefer?
（你喜歡什麼樣的電影？）

B I normally go see scary movies.
（我通常都看恐怖片。）

A Do you like dramas?
（你喜歡劇情片嗎？）

B They're ok if there is some suspense in the plot.
（如果劇情有一點懸疑的話，就還可以。）

A **That's good.**
（那就好。）

It is always nice to see a variety of movies.
（看不同種類的電影是件不錯的事。）

Would you like to see Nightmare on Elm Street?
（你想看「半夜鬼上床」嗎？）

B **Oh, sure.** That is one of my favorite movies.
（好啊，那是我最喜歡的電影之一。）

I have seen it 10 times!
（我看過 10 遍了。）

A It is playing at the Mega Plex Theatre this weekend only.
（只有這個週末在 Mega Plex 戲院有上映呢。）

B Let's go at 9:00pm this Saturday.
（一起去看這週末晚間九點鐘那場吧。）

I would go earlier, but I have to work all day.
（我實在很想早點去，但我整天都要上班。）

A That's okay.
（沒關係。）

I would rather go later than earlier anyway.
（反正我比較想晚點去。）

B Ok. Well, I will see you this Saturday.
（好的，那就星期六見了。）

加強練習

➢ That's good.

A: I really love my new pet kitten.

B: That's good. All animals deserve to be loved.

A：我真的很喜歡我新的小貓寵物。

B：那很好啊，所有動物都值得人們寵愛。

➢ Oh, sure.

A: Could you take me to the mall later on?

B: Oh, sure. I have to run errands anyway.

A：你等一下可不可以載我去百貨公司？

B：沒問題，反正我要出去辦事情。

單字

scary [ˈskɛrɪ] 恐怖的

comedy [ˈkɑmədɪ] 喜劇

mystery [ˈmɪstərɪ] ⓝ 神秘；懸疑

prefer [prɪˈfɝ] 較喜歡

normally [ˈnɔrməlɪ] 通常；一般來說

drama [ˈdrɑmə] 戲劇

suspense [səˈspɛns] （電影）懸疑片

plot [plɑt] 情節

variety [vəˈraɪətɪ] ⓝ 多樣的

favorite [ˈfevərɪt] 最喜歡的

deserve [dɪˈzɝv] ⓥ 應得的；得之無愧的

animal [ˈænəml̩] 動物

errand [ˈɛrənd] 雜務事

Unit 5.

What do you think of action films?

（你覺得動作片如何？）

實用例句

- Do you like action films?
  （你喜歡動作片嗎？）

- Did you like the action stunts that were in the movie?
  （你喜歡那部電影裡的特效動作嗎？）

- I really like the car chasing scenes in action films.
  （我真的很喜歡動作片中車子追撞的情景。）

- Tim doesn't like the violence in action movies.
  （提姆不喜歡動作片中的暴力。）

- Judy loves watching movies with lots of action.
  （茱蒂喜歡看動作比較多的片子。）

實用會話

A I haven't seen an action movie in months.
（我好幾個月沒看動作片了。）

B Really?
（真的嗎？）

I go to the movies at least once a week.
（我至少一週看一部電影。）

I saw a great action film last Friday.
（我上星期五看了一部很不錯的動作片。）

A **Awesome.** I love action movies.
（太棒了。我很喜歡動作片。）

Is it still playing?
（那部片子還在上映嗎？）

B Yes. There is a showing tonight at 10:00pm.
（是的，今晚 10 點還有一場。）

Would you like to see it again?
（你想再看一遍嗎？）

A **Of course**.
（好啊。）

I love action films, too.
（我也很喜歡看動作片。）

B Wow, I didn't know that.

（真的嗎，我不知道你也喜歡動作片。）

We should watch more action movies together.

（我們應該更常一塊看動作片。）

A That would be nice.

（這是個好主意。）

B Great.!

（太棒了。）

What time do you want me to pick you up tonight?

（你想要我今晚什麼時候去接你？）

A How about 9:30pm?

（9:30 如何？）

B That's fine.

（這時間不錯。）

See you at 9:30.

（那就 9:30 見了。）

加強練習

➢ Awesome.

A: I made a 100 on my spelling test!

B: Awesome. You studied a lot for that test.

A：我拼字考試考 100 分。

B：太棒了，你為了那個考試準備了很久。

➢ Of Course.

A: Would you baby-sit my little cousin for me?

B: Of course. I love children.

A：你可以幫我照顧我的小表妹嗎？

B：當然，我愛小孩。

單字

action [ˈækʃən] 行動

film [fɪlm] 電影

chase [tʃes] 追逐

scene [sin] 場景

stunt [stʌnt]　特技表演

violence [ˈvaɪələns] 暴力

awesome [ˈɔsəm] （口語）很棒的

spell [spɛl] 拼字

cousin [ˈkʌzn̩] 表兄弟姐妹

Unit

6. Did you like the movie?

（你喜歡這部電影嗎？）

實用例句

- What was your favorite part of the movie?
（你最喜歡電影的哪一部分？）

- The fight scene was the best part of the movie.
（打鬥場景是這部電影最好的部分。）

- I didn't like this movie as much as the original.
（我對這部電影不像我對原著作那麼喜歡。）

- I wish I had gone skating instead of watching that awful movie.
（我真希望我是去溜冰，而不是去看那部糟透了的電影。）

- Janet loved the movie so much that she saw it twice in one day.
（珍娜很喜歡那部電影，所以一天中看了兩次。）

實用會話

A Do you still want to go to the movies tonight?
（你今晚仍想去看電影嗎？）

B Tonight?
（今天晚上？）

I thought we were going tomorrow.
（我以為我們是明天要去看電影。）

A No. The premiere of Legally Blonde is tonight.
（不對，「金髮尤物」的首演是今天晚上。）

We planned to go on opening night.
（我們的計畫是今晚去看首映。）

B Oh. I forgot.
（哎呀，我忘記了。）

I made plans to go shopping tonight.
（我今晚要去購物。）

A Well, I guess we could go tomorrow.
（這樣的話，我們可以明天再去看。）

B I would love to go with you tomorrow.
（我很樂意明天和你一起去看電影。）

I am sorry about the mishap.
（很抱歉我沒弄清楚狀況。）

A **It's cool.**
（沒關係的。）

I will call you tomorrow when I am on my way.
（我要去的時候，會打電話給你。）

B Excellent.
（太好了。）

A Have fun shopping.
（好好去購物一番吧。）

B Thanks. I will.
（我會的，謝謝。）

加強練習

➢ Excellent.

A: I brought extra snacks for the party.
B: Excellent. I was just about to run out of cookies.

A：我為宴會帶了些點心來。
B：太棒了，餅乾都快吃光了。

➢ It's cool.

A: I am sorry about forgetting your birthday.
B: It's cool. It's not a big deal.

A：抱歉我忘了你的生日。

B：沒關係，這沒什麼大不了。

單字

part [pɑrt] 部份

scene [sin] 場景

fight [faɪt] 爭吵

original [əˈrɪdʒənḷ] 原創作品

awful [ˈɔfʊl] ⓐ 很糟的

twice [twaɪs] 兩次

premiere [prɪˈmɪr] 首次公演

forgot [fɚˈgɑt] 忘記（forget 的過去式）

mishap [ˈmɪshæp] 不幸事故

excellent [ˈɛksələnt] 很棒的

extra [ˈɛkstrə] 額外的；多餘的

snack [snæk] 點心

deal [dil]（口語）事情

Unit 7.

Movie review.

（電影影評）

實用例句

- What would you rate the movie on a scale of 1 to 10?
  （從 1 到 10 來打分數，你給這部電影打幾分？）

- The movie critic gave Titanic a four star rating.
  （電影影評家給「鐵達尼號」四顆星的評價。）

- What do you guys think about that new movie?
  （你們覺得這部新電影如何？）

- Did Charles enjoy watching Pretty Woman?
  （查爾斯喜歡「麻雀變鳳凰」嗎？）

- The critics loved the new movie with Tom Cruise.
  （電影影評家喜歡湯姆克魯斯的新片。）

實用會話

A I hope William enjoys the new movie.
（我希望威廉會喜歡這部新電影。）

B Me, too. I think he really enjoys action films.
（我也是，我想他真的很喜歡動作片。）

A Can you ask him if he wants to go see it?
（你能不能問問看他是否想去看這部電影？）

B What for?
（為什麼要這樣問呢？）

A Well, a group of us is going to go watch it later.
（因為我們一群人再晚一點要一起去看這部電影。）

I was wondering if he'd like to come, too.
（不知道他會不會想要一起去？）

B **Okay**.
（好啊。）

I will ask him for you.
（我幫你問他。）

A **Great.** Thank you.
（太棒了，謝謝你。）

B What time are you guys going?
（你們幾點要去？）

A We will probably leave in an hour.
（我們大概一個小時後會出發。）

B Cool. Have fun.
（太棒了，要好好玩喔。）

A Thanks, we will.
（我們會的，謝謝。）

This movie is probably going to be good.
（這部電影應該很不錯。）

加強練習

➢ Okay.

A: I am going to dinner with Steve.

B: Okay. Bring me back a to-go order.

A：我要和史帝夫一起共進晚餐。

B：好啊，幫我外帶一份晚餐。

➢ Great.

A: Suzy won first place at the dance recital.

B: Great. I'll put in the school paper.

A：蘇西在舞蹈公演得到第一名。

B：太棒了，我會把這消息登在校刊上。

單字

review [rɪ'vju] 審核

scale [skel] ⓝ 等級

rating ['retɪŋ] 等級

critic ['krɪtɪk] 影評家

wonder ['wʌndɚ] 想；想知道

probably ['prɑbəblɪ] 或許；可能的

fun [fʌn] 好玩；樂趣

recital [rɪ'saɪtl̩] 表演會

Unit

8. Renting a videotape.

（租錄影帶）

實用例句

- Do you have a Blockbuster video card?
  （你有百視達卡嗎？）

- What movie should I rent?
  （我應該租哪部電影？）

- I have a coupon to rent a free movie.
  （我有一張免費租片的優待卷。）

- I am renting a horror movie tonight for the slumber party.
  （我為今晚大家來過夜租了一部恐怖電影。）

- Have you turned in the movie rental yet?
  （你還那部租來的片子了嗎？）

實用會話

A What do you want to do tonight?
（你今晚想做什麼？）

B Let's rent movie.
（租部電影吧。）

A Great idea.
（這主意不錯。）

What movie would you like to rent?
（你想租哪一部電影？）

B We can rent Halloween parts one and two.
（我們可以租萬聖節第一集和第二集。）

Those two are my all-time favorites.
（這兩部電影是我的最愛。）

A **Fantastic.** Those are great movies to rent.
（太棒了，這兩部都是租片的好選擇。）

Do you have a movie rental card?
（你有租電影的卡嗎？）

B Yes. It is in my purse.
（有，在我皮包裡。）

I will go get it.
（我去拿。）

A Thanks.
（謝啦。）

B **Wow.** This night is going to be fun.
（哇，今天晚上會很好玩。）

A I hope I remember to buy popcorn.
（我希望我會記得買爆米花。）

B I will call you and remind you to pick some up.
（我會打電話提醒你去買。）

加強練習

➢ Fantastic

A: I ordered two dozen roses as a surprise for Halle.

B: Fantastic! Roses are her favorite.

A：我訂了兩打玫瑰要給海兒一份驚喜。

B：好棒，她最喜歡玫瑰了。

➢ Wow

A: Wow! Look at the beautiful artwork.

B: I know. Museums have great works of art on display.

A：哇！看看這美麗的藝術作品。

B：我知道，博物館展示許多很棒的藝術作品。

單字

rent [rɛnt] 出租；租金

free [fri] ⓐ 免費的

coupon [ˈkupɑn] 折價券

slumber [ˈslʌmbɚ] 睡眠

slumber party 有過夜的宴會

rental [ˈrɛntl̩] 出租

remember [rɪˈmɛmbɚ] 記得

fantastic [fænˈtæstɪk] （口語）好極了；太美妙了

purse [pɝs] 皮包

remind [rɪˈmaɪnd] 提醒

order [ˈɔrdɚ] ⓥ 訂購；訂貨

artwork [ˈɑrtwɝk] 藝術作品

display [dɪsˈple] ⓥ ⓝ 展示；陳列

Unit 9. Talking about the movies.

（討論電影）

實用例句

- What is the best comedy you've ever seen?
（你看過最棒的喜劇是哪部？）

- Justin loves watching old movies.
（賈斯丁喜歡看老片。）

- Kim and I are going to the drive-in movie tonight.
（金和我今晚要去露天劇院看電影。）

- What is the name of the movie that stars Halle Berry?
（海兒貝瑞主演的那部電影叫什麼名字？）

- I went to my first movie when I was 10 years old.
（我十歲時看第一部電影。）

實用會話

A I am tired of seeing the same old movies.
（我厭倦了總是看同樣的老片子。）

The last five movies I saw were boring and had similar plots.
（我最近看的五部片子都很無聊，劇情都很相近。）

B I just went to see a really great movie last week.
（我上週才剛去看過一部好片。）

A **Oh, really?** Which one was that?
（真的嗎？哪一部？）

B It was called Scary Movie 3.
（驚悚第三集。）

A **Ugh!** That movie was not good at all!
（那部電影一點也不好看。）

B How can you say that?
（你怎麼那麼說呢？）

A Well, it had a weak story line.
（這部片的情節很糟。）

It wasn't even scary.
（甚至不很恐怖。）

B The movie was meant to be funny.
（這部電影本來是走詼諧路線的。）

A Well, I thought it was stupid.
（我覺得這是一部很蠢的電影。）

B That is your opinion, but millions find it funny.
（這是你的想法，但許多人覺得它很好笑。）

加強練習

➢ Oh, really?

A: Jason asked Tonya to the dance.

B: Oh, really? I thought he was going to ask Emily.

A：傑森邀請唐雅去參加舞會。

B：真的嗎？我以為他會邀請愛蜜莉。

➢ Ugh!

A: There is a bug in your drink.

B: Ugh! I hate it when that happens.

A：你的飲料裡有蟲子。

B：啊！我最討厭這種事了。

單字

similar [ˈsɪmələ˞] 相似的

boring [ˈborɪŋ] 乏味的

weak [wik] ⓐ 弱的

funny [ˈfʌnɪ] 奇怪的；滑稽

opinion [əˈpɪnjən] 意見

bug [bʌg] 小蟲

Unit 10. Dollar theater.

（二輪電影院）

實用例句

- I want to go to the dollar theater.
  （我想去看二輪電影院。）

- Can you take me to see Freaky Friday at the dollar theater?
  （你能不能帶我去二輪電影院看辣媽辣妹？）

- The dollar theater still charges a lot at the concession stands.
  （一元電影院的院內點心吧台仍然很貴。）

- I only have enough money to go to the dollar theater.
  （我的錢只夠去一元電影院看電影。）

- I hope Julie can pick us up from the dollar theater.
  （我希望茱莉可以到二輪電影院來接我們。）

美語休閒站

美國二輪電影院的收費大都是美金一塊錢，兩部同映，雖然有些地區，例如：美國東北角的二輪電影院已經漲價到美金一塊半，但是，美國人仍然稱二輪電影院為 dollar theater。

實用會話

A Mona Lisa Smile is playing at the dollar theater.
（蒙娜麗莎的微笑現在正在二輪電影院上映。）

Do you want to go see it?
（你想要去看嗎？）

B **Sure**. I love Julia Roberts.
（當然，我愛死茱莉亞羅伯茲了。）

A **Cool.** What time would you like to go?
（太棒了，你什麼時候想去？）

B Let's go at 4:00 pm.
（我們去看下午 4 點那場吧。）

A Great. I can meet you there.
（好啊，我到那裡去和你會面吧。）

B Could Jan go with us?
（珍可以和我們一起去嗎？）

A Sure. Does she have a dollar?

（當然可以，她有美金一塊錢嗎？）

B I think so.

（我想應該有吧。）

A Well, if she doesn't, I can buy her ticket.

（這樣吧，如果她沒有錢的話，我會替她買票。）

B Okay. I will bring her with me.

（好吧，我會帶她一起去。）

加強練習

➢ Sure

A: Can I take Emma with me to the park?

B: Sure. She loves playing on the swings.

A：我可以帶艾瑪去公園嗎？

B：當然可以，她喜歡玩鞦韆。

➢ Cool

A: I just bought a new DVD player.

B: Cool. I am saving up for one.

A：我剛買了新的 DVD 放影機。

B：棒極了，我正在存錢要買一部呢。

單字

charge [tʃɑrdʒ] ⓥ 收費

enough [ɪ'nʌf] 足夠的

ticket ['tɪkɪt] 票

park [pɑrk] 公園

swings [swɪŋz] 鞦韆

save [sev] 節省

CHAPTER 2

SHOPPING

購物

Unit 1. Go shopping.

（購物）

實用例句

- I enjoy going shopping on the weekends.
  （我喜歡週末時去購物。）

- Do you want to go to the mall and do some shopping?
  （你想要去購物中心買東西嗎？）

- Jan has tons of grocery shopping to do this week.
  （珍這週有許多東西得要買。）

- Have you seen my shopping list?
  （你有沒有看到我的購物清單？）

- Where do you like to go shopping?
  （你想去哪裡買東西呢？）

實用會話

A Did Jake and Amber go shopping?
（捷克和安柏有去購物嗎？）

B Yes, they went last week.
（有，他們上星期去了。）

A Where did they go?
（他們去哪裡購物？）

B They went to the mall and then to a couple of shoe stores.
（他們去購物中心，然後去了幾家鞋店。）

A **Cool.** I love going shopping, but I can't until I get my paycheck.
（真酷，我喜歡去購物，但是我得等領到薪水再說。）

Would you like to go shopping with me next weekend?
（下個週末你想跟我去購物嗎？）

B **Wow.** I would love to go.
（哇，我想去。）

I need a new blouse for school.
（我需要一件新的上衣上學時穿。）

A Okay. We can go to Macy's.
（好的，我們可以去梅西百貨。）

B Could we also go to Banana Republic?
（我們也可以去 Banana Republic 嗎？）

They always have nice blouses.
（他們總是有很棒的上衣。）

A Sure. We can go to several stores.
（好啊，有好幾個商店我們可以去。）

B Great. I will talk to you later.
（好棒，稍後再跟你談。）

加強練習

➢ Cool

A: I got accepted into the National Honor Society today.

B: Cool. That will look good on your resume.

A：今天國家榮譽學會讓我入會。

B：棒極了，這資格在履歷表上會很好看。

➢ Great

A: I went to the gym today for a workout.

B: Great. a morning workout is a nice way to start out the day.

A：我今天去體育館健身。

B：很好啊，早上健身是開始新一天的好方法。

單字

weekend [ˈwikˈɛnd] ⓝ 週末

mall [mɔl] 大型購物中心

grocery [ˈgrosərɪ] 雜貨

tons of 許多

list [lɪst] 明細表

store [stor] ⓝ 商店

paycheck [ˈpe͵tʃɛk] 薪水

blouse [blaʊs] 上衣

several [ˈsɛvrəl] 幾個

accept [əkˈsɛpt] vt. 接受

resume [͵rɛzʊˈme] 履歷表

gym [dʒɪm] 健身房

workout [ˈwɝk͵aʊt] 運動

Unit 2. Sales

（大減價）

實用例句

- Do you know if Sears has anything on sale?
（你知道席爾斯百貨有特價嗎？）

- There is a back to school sale on school supplies at Wal-Mart next week.
（Wal-Mart 下週在文具用品方面，有開學大減價的優惠。）

- I am going to see if Old Navy has any clearance sales.
（我想去 Old Navy 看看有沒有清倉大拍賣。）

- I only buy clothes when they are on sale.
（我只有在衣服打折時，才會進行購買。）

- Target is having a "One Day Sale," and everything is 10% off.
（Target 現在有「一日特價」的活動，每件東西都打九折。）

實用會話

A I haven't gone shopping in months.

（我好幾個月沒有購物了。）

B You should go to the mall.

（你應該去購物中心走走。）

At least 10 stores are having their clearance sales right now.

（至少有十家店現在都在清倉拍賣。）

A **Wow!** I bet I could find a lot of bargains.

（哇，我打賭我可以找到許多不錯的東西。）

B Oh, sure.

（那當然。）

You could find things priced up to 50% off the regular price.

（你甚至可以找到打五折的商品呢。）

A **Awesome.** I am going to go next week.

（太棒了，我下週就去購物。）

B Oh, no. You should go this week before all of the good merchandise is sold.

（這樣不行，你應該要這個月去，要不然所有好東西都被賣光了。）

These sales last a while, but the good things

go quickly.
（這些銷售都會持續好一陣子，但好東西都賣的比較快。）

A Well, I guess I should go tomorrow then.
（這樣的話，我想我應該明天去。）

B Yes, you should go as soon as possible to get the best deals.
（是的，你應該盡快去，才可以得到好的交易。）

A Thanks for telling me about the great sales.
（謝謝你告訴我這些好買賣。）

B You're welcome.
（不客氣。）

Happy shopping!
（購物愉快了。）

加強練習

➢ Wow

A: I finished stacking all 100 sets of books.
B: Wow! You are a fast worker.

A：我剛剛疊完 100 套書。
B：哇，你工作好快啊。

➢ Awesome.

A: I met a really nice guy at the coffee house.

B: Awesome. It's hard to find nice guys these days.

A：我在咖啡店認識了一個很不錯的男生。

B：太棒了，現在要認識不錯的男生已經很不容易了。

單字

sale [sel] 拍賣

supply [sə'plaɪ] 供應

clearance ['klɪrəns] 清倉

bargain ['bɑrgɪn] ⓝ 便宜貨；划算的

regular ['rɛgjələ˞] 普通的

merchandise ['mɝtʃən,daɪz] 貨物

quickly ['kwɪklɪ] 很快地

last [læst] v. 延續；持續

possible ['pɑsəbḷ] ⓐ可能的

deal [dil] 交易

Unit 3. Trying on clothes: the size

（試穿衣服：尺寸）

實用例句

- Can I help you with that?
  （有什麼我能幫忙的嗎？）

- Do you have this dress in a size 5?
  （這件洋裝有 5 號的尺寸嗎？）

- I can never find jeans in the right size.
  （我永遠也找不到理想尺寸的牛仔褲。）

- Suzy has to exchange her dress for a larger size.
  （蘇茜想要將洋裝換大一號的尺寸。）

- Do you think that I should try a smaller size shirt?
  （你覺得我應不應該試試小一點尺寸的襯衫。）

實用會話

A I hate trying on clothes!
（我好討厭試穿衣服。）

I can never seem to find the right size no matter how hard I try.
（我好像不管怎麼努力嘗試，永遠都找不到適合的尺寸。）

B You should ask a store associate for help.
（你應該請店裡的人員協助你。）

They are experts at things like that.
（她們是這方面的專家。）

A **That's okay.**
（算了，沒關係。）

The associates try to get you to buy things you don't need.
（店員只會嘗試要你去買那些你不需要的東西。）

B That is not always true.
（事情並不總是這樣。）

A Well, I am having trouble deciding on the size 5 or size 7 skirt.
（我決定不了裙子應該要拿 5 號還是 7 號？）

B They both seemed to fit nicely when you tried them on.
（當你試穿時，好像兩件都很適合你。）

A I know. That is the problem.
（我知道，問題就在這裡。）

Which do you think I should buy?
（你覺得我應該要買哪一件才好呢？）

B I would buy the size 7.
（我會買 7 號。）

If it is too big, it will shrink after a few washes.
（如果太大，洗幾次後就會縮水了。）

A **Good idea.**
（這主意不錯。）

If the size 5 shrinks after a few washes, it might become too small.
（如果 5 號在洗幾次後縮水的話，就可能會變得太小件了。）

B That's right. Go for the size 7.
（沒錯，就買 7 號好了。）

加強練習

➢ That's okay.

A: Would you like some help with your chores?

B: That's okay. I can manage them by myself.

A：你要人幫你做這些事嗎？

B：沒關係，我可以自己來。

➢ Good idea.

A: Next time, we should all go out as a group.

B: Good idea. The more the merrier.

A：下次我們應該大家一起出去。

B：這主意不錯，越多人越好玩。

單字

size [saɪz] 大小；尺碼

right [raɪt] (adj) 正確

exchange [ɪks'tʃendʒ] 交換

try on 試穿

seem [sim] 似乎

hard [hɑrd] 努力的

associate [ə'soʃɪˌet] 同事

expert ['ɛkspɚt] (n) 專家

trouble ['trʌbl̩] 麻煩；困難

problem ['prɑbləm] 問題

shrink [ʃrɪŋk] 縮水

manage ['mænɪdʒ] 設法做到

merry ['mɛrɪ] 快樂的

Unit 4. Trying on clothes: the style

（試穿衣服：款式）

實用例句

- What style of jeans do you like to wear?
  （你喜歡穿什麼樣子的牛仔褲？）

- I want to try on a different style of shoes.
  （我想要試試不同樣式的鞋子。）

- Jenny loves trying on stylish clothes.
  （珍妮很喜歡嘗試時髦的衣服。）

- Todd prefers wearing suits instead of sports jackets.
  （塔德比較喜歡穿西裝，而非運動夾克。）

- Jacob tried on a different style of pants, but he liked his old pair better.
  （雅各試了不同樣式的褲子，但他還是比較喜歡舊的那件。）

實用會話

A What style of blouse do you prefer?
（你比較喜歡怎樣的上衣？）

B I like blouses with buttons.
（我喜歡有釦子的上衣。）

They look more professional.
（看起來比較專業。）

A I was going to try on this pullover blouse.
（我本來要試穿這件套頭上衣的。）

B It is nice, but it doesn't look as professional as the button-up.
（看起來不錯，但不像有鈕釦的那件那麼專業。）

A **That's true.**
（這倒是真的。）

I will try on both and make a decision.
（我會兩件都試穿看看，再做決定。）

B That is a good idea.
（那是個好主意。）

A I really like the pullover blouse.
（我真的比較喜歡那件套頭的。）

Which did you like?
（你比較喜歡哪件呢？）

B I actually liked the pullover blouse better, too.
（事實上，我也比較喜歡那件套頭的。）

A I guess button-up blouses aren't always the best.
（我想鈕釦型的上衣並不一定是最好的。）

B **Right.**
（這話一點也不錯。）

Maybe it depends on who is wearing the blouse.
（也許要看看穿的人是誰。）

加強練習

➢ That's true.

A: Next time you want to borrow my shirt, you should ask.

B: That's true. I am sorry for not asking you the first time.

A：下次如果你想借我的襯衫，你應該先詢問我。

B：這倒是真的，很抱歉第一次沒有先詢問你。

➢ Right

A: I want Jim to be nicer to his brother.

B: Right. Jim should control his temper.

A：我想讓吉姆對他弟弟好一點。

B：不錯，吉姆應該試著控制自己的脾氣。

單字

wear [wɛr] ⓥ 穿

jeans [dʒinz] 牛仔褲

different [ˈdɪfərənt] ⓐ 不同的

stylish [ˈstaɪlɪʃ] 時髦的

pair [pɛr] 一雙

prefer [prɪˈfɝ] 較喜歡

button [ˈbʌtn̩] ⓝ 釦子；按鈕

professional [prəˈfɛʃənl̩] 專業的

decision [dɪˈsɪʒən] ⓝ 決定

control [kənˈtrol] ⓥ 控制

temper [ˈtɛmpɚ] 脾氣

Unit 5. Trying on clothes: the color
（試穿衣服：顏色）

實用例句

- Should I try on the black dress or the white one?
  （我應該試穿黑色還是白色的洋裝？）
- Jason loves trying on different styles of black pants.
  （杰森很喜歡試試看不同種類的黑褲子。）
- Julie wants to try on the red or the orange dress.
  （茱莉想要試穿看看紅色和橘色的洋裝。）
- Kim can't try on the black dress. It is too small.
  （金不能試穿那件黑色洋裝，因為它太小了。）
- I wonder what color shoes should I try on.
  （我在想我倒底應該試穿什麼顏色的鞋子。）

實用會話

A I don't like the pair of shoes Nickie is trying on.
（我不喜歡妮琪正在試穿的那雙鞋子。）

B What is wrong with them?
（有什麼問題嗎？）

A I don't like the color.
（我不喜歡那個顏色。）

It is an ugly shade of green.
（那種綠色很醜。）

B Well, why don't you tell her?
（那你為什麼不告訴她呢？）

A I am not the one who will be wearing the shoes, so she can try on whatever color she chooses.
（我又不是那個要穿那雙鞋子的人，所以她可以穿任何她想要的顏色。）

B But I think Nickie would appreciate your opinion.
（但我認為妮琪會想要聽聽你的意見。）

Come on. Let her know how you feel.
（來吧，讓她聽聽你的想法。）

A **Oh, all right.**

（好吧。）

I don't think that is a flattering color on you.

（我不認為這個顏色會把妳襯托的更漂亮。）

B What did Nickie say?

（妮琪怎麼說？）

A She told me thanks for my input because she was thinking the same thing.

（她謝謝我的意見，因為她也有同樣的顧慮。）

She is going to buy the black shoes instead.

（她將買黑色的那雙鞋。）

B That's cool. I am glad you spoke up and told her what you were thinking.

（那很好啊，我很高興你把想法告訴了她。）

加強練習

➢ Come on.

A: Come on. Please help me do the dishes.

B: I can't. I have homework to do!

A：來吧，幫我一起洗碗。

B：我沒辦法，我得做功課。

➢ Oh, all right.

A: Will you please make your bed?

B: Oh, all right. I will get to it in a minute.

A：你能不能整理自己的床鋪？

B：好的，我等一下就去整理。

單字

color [ˈkʌlɚ] ⓝ 顏色

shade [ʃed] 色調

ugly [ˈʌglɪ] ⓐ醜的

choose [tʃuz] ⓥ 選擇

wear [wɛr] ⓥ 穿

appreciate [əˈpriʃɪˌet] ⓥ 感激

opinion [əˈpɪnjən] 意見

flatter [flætɚ] 使顯得優點突出

input [ˈɪnpʊt] 意見

Unit

6. Trying on clothes: too expensive

（試穿衣服，太貴）

實用例句

- I am not going to try on clothes that are too expensive.
  （我不想要試穿那些太過昂貴的衣服。）

- Mike likes to try on clothes that are out of his price range.
  （麥克喜歡試穿那些價格他付不起的衣服。）

- Michelle went to try on clothes at Macy's.
  （米雪兒跑去梅茜百貨公司去試穿衣服。）

- Why are you always telling me my clothes are too expensive?
  （你為什麼總告訴我，我的衣服太貴了？）

- Don't try those on; they are too expensive.
  （不要試穿那些衣服，它們太過昂貴了。）

實用會話

A I am going to try this cute black dress on.
（我要去試穿看看這件可愛的黑色洋裝。）

B **Go for it!** That dress is adorable.
（去啊，那件洋裝很可愛呢。）

A I love it!
（我好喜歡這件洋裝。）

But I think it is too expensive.
（可是我覺得它太貴了。）

B I think you should try on something else then.
（我認為妳應該試試看其他件。）

A But it looked really nice on me.
（但我穿上它真的很好看。）

Maybe I will wait for it to go on sale.
（也許我應該等到特價時再買。）

B **Great idea.** In the meantime, you could save your money.
（這主意不錯，同時妳還可以存錢呢。）

A I could, but I am going to buy something now since I am already here.
（對啊，但我既然現在來了，就得買些東西才行。）

B What else are you going to try on?

（妳還要試穿些什麼呢？）

A I am going to try on something that is within my current price range.

（我要試穿一些我預算買得起的東西。）

B That's smart.

（這是聰明的做法。）

Then you won't have to add something else to your "wish list."

（這樣妳就不用把其他事情加到妳的「願望單」中了。）

加強練習

➤ Go for it

A: Should I take a trip to Hawaii?

B: Go for it! That island is a tropical paradise.

A：我應該去夏威夷玩嗎？

B：去啊，那個島嶼是個熱帶天堂呢。

➤ Great idea.

A: I think we should start exercising three times a week.

B: Great idea. We will be healthier and lose

weight.

A：我認為我們應該開始一週運動三次。

B：這是個好主意，這樣我們會更健康，還可以減重。

單字

expensive [ɪk'spɛnsɪv] 昂貴的

price [praɪs] 價格

range [rendʒ] 範圍

cute [kjut] 可愛；漂亮的

adorable [ə'dorəbl̩] 可愛的

save [sev] 節省

else [ɛls] 其他的

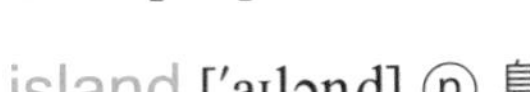

island ['aɪlənd] ⓝ 島

Unit 7.

Items sold out

（東西賣完了）

實用例句

- The store is completely out of blue folders.
（這家店的藍色卷夾全部賣光了。）

- I had to get a rain check for the DVD player at Sears.
（關於席爾斯百貨公司的 DVD 放影機，我得拿一張貨到時仍可享優惠的優待券。）

- I hope they haven't sold out of all of the yellow sweaters.
（我希望他們還沒有賣光黃色的毛衣。）

- I think the store ran out of jeans in size 10.
（我想店裡面 10 號的牛仔褲都賣完了。）

- If the shoes are sold out, we can get a rain check.
（如果鞋子都賣完了，我們就延期再買吧。）

美語休閒站

rain check 是源自棒球等露天球賽，因為下雨必須改期再賽，主辦單位會發給每人一張 rain check，憑券可以等球賽再賽時免費入場，美國的商店如果有打折品時，除非有聲明是限量打折，否則打折品如果賣完時，顧客可以跟商店拿一張 rain check，等貨補齊時，雖然已過打折期限，仍可憑券以打折價錢購買該物品。

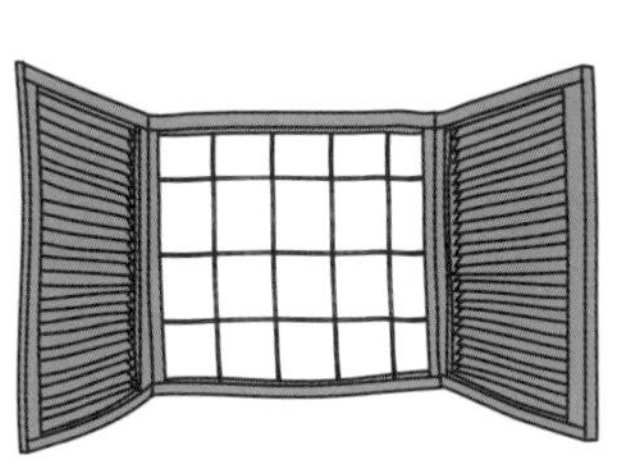

實用會話

A Were you able to get a dozen folders from Office Depot?

（你是否在辦公文具賣場中買到一打的文書夾了呢？）

B No. They were sold out.

（沒有，都賣完了。）

I could only get 4.

（我只買到了 4 個。）

A What did you do about the other 8?

（那另外 8 個怎麼辦呢？）

B I had to go to another office supply store and buy the rest.

（我必須去另外一家文具商店，把數目補齊。）

A Oh. Thanks for going to all the trouble.

（謝謝你這麼麻煩的去買文件夾。）

I didn't think that Office Depot would run out of them.

（我沒想到辦公文具賣場東西會賣完了。）

B **Don't mention it.**

（沒關係。）

The other store was just another block away.

（另外那家店只隔了一條街而已。）

A What about the other supplies?

（那其他的文具呢？）

B **Ugh!** I completely forgot about the other supplies.

（啊，我完全忘了其他文具的事。）

A It's ok.

（沒關係的。）

I will go to Office Depot and pick them up.

（我會再去辦公文具賣場，把它們買齊。）

B Thanks. Sorry about that.
（謝謝，抱歉讓你麻煩了。）

加強練習

➢ Don't mention it.

A: Thanks for letting me spend the night with you.

B: Don't mention it. What are friends for?

A：謝謝妳讓我在妳這裡待了一個晚上。

B：別提這個，要不然要朋友幹嘛。

➢ Ugh!

A: Ugh! I hate cleaning the bathroom.

B: Well, it's a dirty job, but someone's got to do it.

A：啊，我好討厭清理浴室。

B：這是個髒工作，但總要有人做啊。

單字

folder [ˈfoldɚ] 文件夾

completely [kəmˈplitlɪ] 完全地

sweater [ˈswɛtɚ] 毛衣

jeans [dʒinz] 牛仔褲

supply [sə'plaɪ] 供應

rest [rɛst] 其餘的

trouble ['trʌbl̩] 麻煩；困難

block [blɑk] （市區裡）街段

spend [spɛnd] 花（時間）

mention ['mɛnʃən] 提起；談及

dirty ['dɝtɪ] 髒的

Unit

8. Could you hold this for me?

（可以請你替我留著這個東西嗎？）

實用例句

- Excuse me, could you hold these outfits until tomorrow?
  （抱歉，你可不可以幫我保留這些衣服到明天？）

- I am going to put these shoes on hold until this evening.
  （我會保留這些鞋子到今天晚上。）

- How long does this store hold items for customers?
  （這家店可以為客戶保留東西多久？）

- I left my wallet at home. Could you hold these items for a few hours?
  （我把皮夾忘在家裡，你可不可以幫我保留這些項目幾小時？）

• I am sorry, but our store doesn't keep items on hold for longer than 24 hours.
（我很抱歉，但我們的店無法保留東西超過 24 小時。）

實用會話

A I love this outfit!
（我好喜歡這件衣服。）

B Wow. It does look great on you.
（哇，它好適合妳呢。）

How much is it?
（多少錢呢？）

A **Oh, no!**
（不好了。）

It is $150, and I only brought $100 with me.
（這件衣服要 150 元，我只帶了 100 元。）

B Maybe you could put it on hold and go get more money.
（也許你可以請他們幫你保留這件衣服，然後妳可以去領一些錢。）

A That's a good idea.
（這主意不錯。）

I will check with the sales associate.
（我去向店員問問看。）

B Well, what did she say?
（她怎麼說？）

A She said that they can only hold merchandise for up to 3 hours.
（她說她們最多只能保留商品 3 個小時。）

B Cool.
（這很不錯啊。）

That is plenty of time for you to get more money.
（給了妳充裕的時間去領錢。）

A **Exactly.**
（話倒沒錯。）

I am going to run home. I will be right back.
（我要趕快回家去了，我馬上會回來。）

B Okay.
（好的。）

I will stay here and do some more shopping.
（我會在這裡等妳，再買一些東西。）

加強練習

➢ Oh, no!

A: Oh, no! I forgot to take out the garbage.

B: It's okay. I will call home and ask Andy to take it out.

A：唉呀，不好了，我忘了倒垃圾。

B：沒關係的，我會打電話回家，請安迪去丟垃圾。

➢ Exactly.

A: It would be better for us to eat after the movie.

B: Exactly. That way, we won't have to rush.

A：我們最好看完電影再吃飯。

B：這話一點也沒錯，這樣我們就不用太趕了。

單字

hold [hold] 留著

outfit [ˈaʊtˌfɪt] 服裝

item [ˈaɪtəm] 貨品；項目

customer [ˈkʌstəmɚ] ⓝ 顧客

wallet [ˈwɑlɪt] ⓝ 皮包；皮夾子

associate [əˈsoʃɪˌet] 同事

merchandise [ˈmɝtʃənˌdaɪz] 貨物

plenty [ˈplɛntɪ] 很多

exactly [ɪgˈzæktlɪ] 確切的；（加強語氣）正好

garbage [ˈgɑrbɪdʒ] 垃圾

rush [rʌʃ] 急著趕

Unit 9. Coupons

（折價券）

實用例句

- I have a buy-one-get-one-free coupon that expires next week.
  （我有一張買一送一的折價券，下週到期。）

- Do you have any coupons for JC Penny?
  （你有 JC Penny 的折價券嗎？）

- Mike bought two shirts for the price of one with his coupon.
  （麥可用他的折價券，以一件的價格買到兩件襯衫。）

- Old Navy has discount coupons on their website.
  （Old Navy 在它們的網站上有折價券。）

- I am going to look in the newspaper for coupons before I go shopping.
  （我在去買東西前，會先找找看報紙裡面有沒有折價券。）

實用會話

A Have you seen today's newspaper?

（你有沒有看今天的報紙？）

B No, why are you looking for it?

（沒有，你為什麼要找報紙？）

A I want to check for coupons.

（我想找找看有沒有折價券。）

I am going grocery shopping later on.

（我等一下要去雜貨店買東西。）

B **How exciting!**

（真是太令人興奮了。）

Kroger has triples coupons all week.

（Kroger 商店這週有三倍的折價券。）

A **Wow!**

（哇。）

I could save up to three times more if I could find the coupons.

（如果我找到這些折價卷的話，買東西就可以省三倍的錢了。）

B I will help you look for the newspaper.

（我會幫你找報紙。）

A Thanks.

（謝謝。）

Why don't you check the bedrooms?
（你去臥室找看看吧？）

I will look in the kitchen.
（我去廚房找。）

B I found it.
（我找到了。）

The paper was in Sally's bedroom.
（報紙在莎莉的房間。）

A Great.
（太棒了。）

Now I can start clipping coupons.
（現在我可以開始剪折價卷了。）

B We can buy something extra since we will be saving money.
（既然我們可以省錢，就可以買一些其他東西了。）

美語休息站

triples coupons是美國商品的促銷方式之一，美國的廠商會在報紙夾coupon（折價券）讓顧客使用，折價券的面額不一，買該折價券上面的物品時，有些是可以折價美金50分，有些是可以折價美金一塊錢，如果有哪家商店打出triple coumpons的廣告時，那就表示你拿著該廠商出的折價券到該商店購買物品時，可以依照折價的面額，折價三倍，例如：coupon 的面額是可以折價美金 50 分，那麼，那麼你拿著這張 coupon 到該商店去買東西，就可以有美金一塊半的折價。

加強練習

➢ How exciting!

A: Jesse made the football team.

B: How exciting! His parents must be proud of him.

A：傑西終於進了足球隊。

B：真是太令人興奮了，他的父母一定很以他為傲。

➢ Wow!

A: Wow! Look at how fast that little dog is running.

B: He's really fast for being such a small dog!

A：哇，看看那隻小狗跑得多快。

B：對一隻小狗而言，牠真的跑得很快。

單字

coupon [ˈkupɑn] 折價券

expire [ɪkˈspaɪr] 屆期；滿期

discount [ˈdɪskaʊnt] 折扣

newspaper [ˈnjuzˌpepɚ] 報紙

exciting [ɪkˈsaɪtɪŋ] 令人興奮的

later [ˈletɚ] 稍後

triple [ˈtrɪpl̩] 三倍的

check [tʃɛk] ⓥ 查一查

kitchen [ˈkɪtʃən] 廚房

clip [klɪp] 剪

extra [ˈɛkstrə] 額外的；多餘的

team [tim] 隊伍；團隊；一組

proud [praʊd] 感到驕傲

fast [fæst] 快

Unit 10. Refund

（退錢）

實用例句

- I am going to return this cell phone.
  （我想要把這隻手機退掉。）

- Does that store give refunds if you are not satisfied with the product?
  （如果顧客不滿意產品，那家店可不可以退錢？）

- I am going to go to the manager and demand a refund for this malfunctioning product.
  （我要去找經理，要求將這個性能有問題的產品退錢。）

- Did James ever get a refund from that store?
  （詹姆士是否曾經在那家店退過錢？）

- Sears has a great refund policy.
  （席爾斯百貨公司有很棒的退錢規定。）

實用會話

A My CD player broke.
（我的 CD 音響壞了。）

B Haven't you only had it for two days?
（你不是才買了 2 天而已嗎？）

A Yes. I think I should exchange it for another one.
（沒錯，我認為我應該要去換一台新的。）

B Maybe you should think about getting a refund.
（也許你應該考慮請他們退錢。）

A But I need a CD player.
（可是我需要一台 CD 音響。）

B You could always buy another one from a different store.
（你可以到另外一家去買啊。）

A **That's true.**
（這倒是真的。）

I will consider that.
（我會考慮看看。）

Do you know what Target's return policy is?
（你知道 Target 這家店的退錢規定嗎？）

B **Of course.**

（當然。）

You have 10 days to get a full refund on any item.

（買東西的 10 天內，如果要退貨，他們會全額退錢。）

A Do I need to have my receipt?

（我需要把收據帶著嗎？）

B No, but you must have the product's original box and packaging.

（不需要，但你需要把產品放到原來的包裝盒中。）

加強練習

➢ That's true.

A: Allen is a really nice guy.

B: That's true. He is always willing to help.

A：亞倫真是個好人。

B：這倒是真的，他總是很樂意助人。

➢ Of course.

A: Would you please clean out the birdcage?

B: Of course. I have no problem doing that.

A：能否請你清理鳥籠？

B：當然，我可以幫忙。

單字

return [rɪ'tɝn] 歸還；退還

satisfied ['saɪtɪsfaɪd] 滿意的

refund [rɪ'fʌnd] 退款；退貨

demand [dɪ'mænd] ⓥ 要求

manager ['mænɪdʒɚ] 經理

malfunctioning [mɔl'fʌŋkʃənɪŋ] 故障的

product ['prɑdəkt] 產品

policy ['pɑləsɪ] 政策

exchange [ɪks'tʃendʒ] 交換

different ['dɪfərənt] ⓐ 不同的

receipt [rɪ'sit] 收據

original [ə'rɪdʒənl̩] 原本的

really ['riəlɪ] 真的

birdcage ['bɝdkedʒ] 鳥籠

CHAPTER 3

AT THE SCHOOL

學校生活

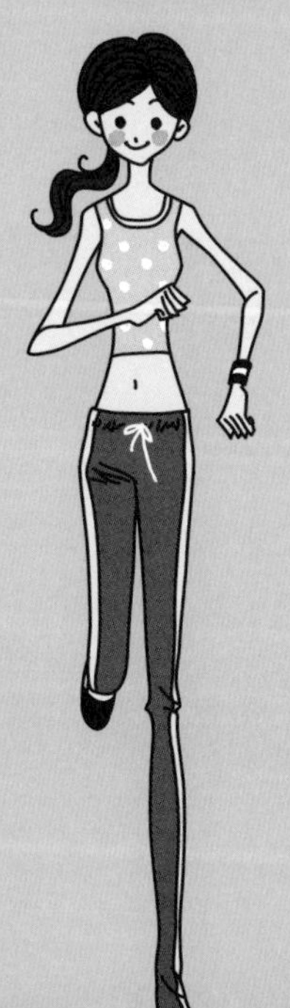

Unit 1. The first day of school.

（開學的第一天）

實用例句

- I always get nervous on the first day of school.
（上學第一天我總是感到緊張。）

- I wonder how many of my friends will be in my new class?
（我好奇會有多少朋友又會與我同班？）

- I am excited about the first day of school.
（我對第一天上學感到興奮。）

- I will get to ride the school bus on the first day of school.
（第一天上學我將坐校車 。）

- I hope I like my new teacher.
（我希望我會喜歡新老師。）

實用會話

A Today was my first day of high school.

（今天是我上中學的第一天。）

B **Wow.** How was it?

（哇，感覺如何？）

A Pretty good.

（還不錯！）

I accidentally went to the wrong class, though.

（雖然我不小心走錯了教室。）

B Were you embarrassed?

（有沒有覺得很尷尬？）

A No, I checked my schedule, and I realized my mistake before the teacher started class.

（沒有，我查了一下課表，在老師開始上課前，就知道自己犯了這個錯誤。）

I was 5 minutes late for my class though.

（所以我遲到了 5 分鐘。）

B Well, 5 minutes isn't too bad. Did you make any new friends?

(5 分鐘還不算太糟糕，你有認識新朋友嗎？）

A Yes. I made some friends at lunch.

（有，午餐時認識一些新朋友。）

We decided to form a study group because we all have the same class schedule.
（因為全部都上同樣的課程，所以我們決定成立一個讀書會。）

B **Excellent.**
（太棒了。）

It sounds like you had a good day.
（你今天聽起來過得不錯。）

A Yeah.
（是啊。）

I think I will enjoy high school.
（我想我會喜歡中學生活。）

B That's great.
（太好了。）

I am glad you enjoyed your day.
（很高興你今天過的很愉快。）

加強練習

➢ Wow.

A: The bank I was at got robbed today.

B: Wow! Are you okay?

A：我去的銀行今天被搶了。

B：哇，你沒事吧？

➢ Excellent.

A: Judy finished her art project.

B: Excellent. I can't wait to see how she does in the art competition.

A：茱蒂剛完成了她的美術作品。

B：太好了，我等不及要看她在藝術競賽的表現。

單字

nervous [ˈnɝvəs] 緊張的

excited [ɪkˈsaɪtɪd] 感到興奮的

ride [raɪd] 搭載；搭乘

accidentally [ˌæksəˈdɛntḷɪ] (adv) 意外地

embarrassed [ɪmˈbærəst] 難為情

mistake [məˈstek] (n) 錯誤

schedule [ˈskɛdʒʊl] 課程表

though [ðo] （口語）不過

group [grup] (n) 一群人

excellent [ˈɛksələnt] 很棒的

rob [rɑb] 搶劫

competition [kɑpəˈtɪʃən] 競爭

Unit 2. Lunch time.

（吃午餐）

實用例句

- I can't wait until lunch.
  （我等不及要吃午餐了。）

- I always bring a tuna salad for lunch.
  （我的午餐帶的都是鮪魚沙拉。）

- Do you know what they are serving at lunch today?
  （你知道他們今天的午餐是什麼嗎？）

- I love pizza day at school.
  （我喜歡吃學校的披薩餐。）

- I forgot my lunch at home. I will have to borrow lunch money from someone.
  （我把便當忘在家裡，必須向別人借錢吃午餐。）

實用會話

A I'm hungry. I can't wait until lunch to eat.
（我好餓，等不到吃午餐的時候了。）

B Why don't you go to the snack machine?
（為什麼不去點心販賣機買點東西吃呢？）

A I don't have any money.
（我沒帶錢。）

B Well, how are you going to eat lunch?
（那你午餐怎麼辦？）

A I brought my lunch.
（我有帶午餐。）

By the way, can I borrow some change?
（對了，可以借點零錢嗎？）

B Sure. Why?
（沒問題，不過你要作什麼呢？）

A Great! **I decided to buy a snack after all.**
（太棒了！我還是決定要買點零食。）

What should I get?
（該買些什麼呢？）

B I think you should get some chips.
（我想你應該買些洋芋片。）

A That's a good choice.
（那是不錯的選擇。）

B **Right.**
（沒錯。）

It should keep you full until lunchtime.
（這樣到午餐前，你都不會餓了。）

加強練習

➢ Great

A: Emily made straight A's for the entire semester.

B: Great. She is such a dedicated student.

A：愛蜜莉整個學期都拿全 A。

B：太棒了，她真是個認真的好學生。

➢ Right

A: I believe that children should listen to their parents.

B: Right. Children can learn a lot through obedience.

A：我覺得孩童應該聽父母的話。

B：沒錯，孩童能夠由服從中學到許多東西。

單字

borrow ['bɑro] ⓥ 借用

machine [mə'ʃin] 機器

change [tʃendʒ] ⓝ 零錢；小額硬幣

snack [snæk] 點心

choice [tʃɔɪs] ⓝ 選擇

straight [stret] 連續的

semester [sə'mɛstɚ] 學期

dedicated ['dɛdɪˌketɪd] 一心一意的；專注的；很投入的

obedience [ə'bidɪəns] 服從

Unit 3. Final exams.

（期末考試）

實用例句

- Have you studied for your final exams?
（你期末考準備好了嗎？）

- I have two final exams and a research paper.
（我有兩科考試和一份研究報告。）

- Would you help me study for final exams?
（你可以協助我準備期末考嗎？）

- There are three more weeks until final exams.
（還有三個多星期就要期末考了。）

- How many final exams do you have to take?
（期末考你要考幾科？）

實用會話

A I have three final exams on Friday.
（我星期五有三科期末考。）

I am so stressed out about them.
（我覺得壓力好大。）

B **How awful!**
（好可怕！）

I am sorry that you have to have three in one day.
（我同情你一天內要考三科。）

A I'm worried that I won't be able to study enough for them.
（我擔心對這些科目的準備會不夠。）

There aren't enough hours in a day.
（一天 24 小時是不夠的。）

B I suggest you manage your time better to get all that studying in.
（我建議你好好安排，善加利用時間讀書。）

A That's true.
（這倒是真的。）

Got any ideas?
（有其它建議嗎？）

B You can study in the morning before class.
（你早上上課前可以讀書。）

Do you have a part time job?
（你有兼職工作嗎？）

A Yes. I work at McDonald's.
（有，我在麥當勞打工。）

B You should take your notes and study during your breaks.
（你應該帶著筆記，趁休息時唸書。）

A **Cool.**
（太酷了，這主意不錯。）

I never thought about doing that.
（我從沒想到這樣做。）

B Good luck on your exams.
（祝你考試好運。）

I know you will pass them all.
（我知道你可以順利過關的。）

加強練習

➢ How awful!

A: I pricked my finger sewing today.

B: How awful. Does it still hurt?

A：今天我在裁縫時，刺到手指了。

B：太可怕了，還很痛嗎？

➢ Cool.

A: I want you to come to my birthday party.

B: Cool. Thanks for inviting me.

A：我希望你來參加我的生日宴會。

B：太棒了，謝謝你的邀請。

單字

final [ˈfaɪnḷ] 最後的

exam [ɪgˈzæm] 考試（examination 的縮寫）

research [rɪˈsɝtʃ] 研究

paper [ˈpepɚ] 研究報告

stressed [strɛst] 有壓力的

awful [ˈɔfʊl] ⓐ 很糟的；可怕的

manage [ˈmænɪdʒ] 設法做到

job [dʒɑb] 工作；職位；職務

luck [lʌk] 運氣

prick [prɪk] 刺

Unit 4. Extracurricular activities.

（課外活動）

實用例句

- Does Tommy play any sports for the high school?
（湯米在高中有參加運動項目嗎？）

- I am trying out for the school cheerleading squad.
（我想試試看加入學校啦啦隊。）

- Suzy is president of the student council.
（蘇茜是學生會主席。）

- Jake is running for senior class president.
（傑克正在競選畢聯會主席。）

- What extracurricular activities should I participate in?
（我應該參加什麼課外活動？）

實用會話

A I am always so bored after school.
（下課後我總是很無聊。）

B You should join a school club or sports team.
（你應該參加學校社團或運動團隊。）

A I can't play sports, so maybe I will join a club.
（我不擅長運動，也許應該參加社團。）

B What interests do you have?
（你的興趣是什麼？）

A I like to write poetry.
（我喜歡寫詩。）

B **Splendid.**
（很棒呀！）

You should join the school literary society.
（你應該加入文學社。）

A Do you know when they meet?
（你知道他們的聚會時間嗎？）

B No, but you can check the bulletin boards.
（不知道，但你可以查看公佈欄。）

A **Great idea.**
（好主意。）

Now maybe I won't be so bored anymore.
（也許這樣我就不會再這麼無聊了。）

B There are plenty of extracurricular activities here, so you should never be bored.
（這兒有許多的社團活動，你應該再也不會感到無聊了。）

加強練習

➢ Splendid

A: I found the recipe for fried chicken.

B: Splendid. We can have that for dinner this Saturday.

A：我找到了烤雞的食譜。

B：太好了，我們星期六晚餐就吃這個吧。

➢ Great idea

A: How about we go up to Mt. Vernon for a brisk hike?

B: Great idea. The mountain air is so fresh this time of year.

A：我們到佛能山去爬山如何？

B：好主意，每年這個時候，山上的空氣總是很清新。

單字

extracurricular [ɛkstrəkə'rɪkjələ˞] 課外的

activity [æk'tɪvətɪ] ⓝ 活動

cheerleading ['tʃɪrlidɪŋ] 啦啦隊

squad [skwɑd] 小隊

council ['kaʊnsḷ] 委員會

participate [pə˞'tɪsəpet] 參加

bored [bord] 無聊的

poetry ['poɪtrɪ] 詩

splendid ['splɛndɪd] 極好的

literary ['lɪtərɛrɪ] 文學的

bulletin board 布告欄

recipe ['rɛsəpɪ] 食譜

brisk [brɪsk] 輕快的

hike [haɪk] 徒步旅行

Unit 5. Homework.

（家庭作業）

實用例句

- Did you write down today's algebra homework?
（你寫完了今天的代數作業了嗎？）

- Sandy doesn't do her homework until the day it is due.
（珊蒂不到作業到期，是不會做作業的。）

- I forgot about the English homework.
（我忘記要做英文作業。）

- Billy turned his homework in late, and got 10 points deducted.
（比利遲教作業，所以被扣了 10 分。）

- I hope my homework is correct.
（我希望我的作業寫對了。）

實用會話

A Did Ms. Watson give any homework today?

（華森老師今天有派家庭作業嗎？）

B Yes, we have a 10-page paper due next week.

（有，共有 10 頁報告下週要交。）

A That's all?

（只有這些嗎？）

I was afraid we would have more.

（我還有怕有更多呢。）

B A 10-page paper is a lot of work.

（10 頁報告已經很多了。）

What were you expecting?

（你原本以為還有什麼呢？）

A I was expecting a paper and a reading assignment.

（我原本等著一份報告和閱讀作業。）

B Well, the paper has to be about Romeo and Juliet.

（報告和「羅蜜歐與茱麗葉」有關。）

If you haven't read that, you will need to do that first.

（如果你還沒有讀過，就必須先把它讀完。）

A **Oh, no!** I haven't read it yet.
（喔！糟了！我還沒讀過這個故事。）

I was afraid of this!
（我就擔心會這樣。）

B I'm sorry.
（抱歉。）

I should have been more specific about the assignment.
（對於指派的作業，我早該講明確一點。）

A **That's okay.**
（沒有關係。）

I still have a week to prepare.
（我還有一星期可以準備。）

B That's true.
（這倒是真的。）

Good luck on your paper.
（祝你儘快完成報告。）

加強練習

➢ Oh, no!

A: I lost the gold bracelet you bought for me!

B: Oh, no! I paid $500 for that!

A：我把你買給我的金手鐲弄丟了。

B：真糟糕！它花了我 500 元美金。

➤ That's okay.

A: Would you like another cup of coffee?

B: That's okay. I'm trying to cut down.

A：你想再喝一杯咖啡嗎？

B：不用了，謝謝，我試著要少喝點咖啡。

單字

algebra ['ældʒəbrə] 代數

deduct [dɪ'dʌkt] 扣除；減去

point [pɔɪnt] ⓝ

correct [kə'rɛkt] ⓐⓓⓙ 正確的

assignment [ə'saɪnmənt] ⓝ 作業

afraid [ə'fred] ⓐ 恐怕

specific [spɪ'sɪfɪk] 特定的

prepare [prɪ'pɛr] 準備

bracelet ['breslɪt] 手鐲

CHAPTER 4

Vacation
度假、休假

Unit 1. Vacation plans.

（度假計畫）

實用例句

- Let's go to Mexico for summer vacation.
  （暑假時， 一起去墨西哥旅遊吧。）

- I am scheduled to take a 10-day vacation next month.
  （下個月我計劃休 10 天假。）

- I need a vacation. I am tired of working long hours.
  （我需要休個假，我厭倦了長時間的工作。）

- I wish I could take a trip to Disney World.
  （我希望能夠到迪士尼樂園去旅行。）

- What are our travel plans for this winter?
  （我們今年冬天計劃去哪裏旅行？）

實用會話

A Are you busy?
（你在忙嗎？）

B I am working on an assignment.
（我正在寫作業。）

Is there something you needed?
（你需要幫忙嗎？）

A Well, I want to talk about our vacation plans.
（我想跟你討論我們的旅遊計劃。）

B What about them?
（說來聽聽。）

We are going to Jamaica, right?
（我們要去牙買加，是吧？）

A Yes, but we need to plan where we will stay and what airline to use.
（是的，但我們需要計畫討論食宿與航班細節。）

B That's true.
（這倒是。）

Could we talk about it tomorrow?
（我們可以明天再討論這個嗎？）

A I would rather make the plans as soon as possible.
（如果可能，我想儘早做計畫。）

We might miss out on a better deal if we wait.
（如果等太久，可能會失去比較好的價格。）

B **Okay.**
（好吧。）

Let's talk about it now, then.
（那現在就來討論吧。）

A **Great.**
（太好了。）

I was thinking we could go online to check out airfares and hotel specials.
（我想我們可以上網查查，看看機票費用與住宿優惠。）

B Cool. We can use my laptop.
（太好了，我們可以用我的筆記型電腦來查。）

加強練習

➢ Okay.

A: We should quit arguing and come to an agreement.

B: Okay. What do you suggest we do then?

A：我們應該快達成協議，不要再爭論了。

B：好的，你建議我們該怎麼做。

➢ Great.

A: I have an idea for the project.

B: Great. Let's talk about it over lunch.

A：我對這個專案有個意見。

B：太好了，我們午餐時一起討論吧。

單字

vacation [və'keʃən] ⓝ休假；假期

schedule ['skɛdʒʊl] ⓥ安排（時間）

tired [taɪrd] 疲倦的

trip [trɪp] 旅程；旅遊

plan [plæn] 計畫

possible ['pɑsəbḷ] ⓐ可能的

deal [dil] 交易

airfare ['ɛr,fɛr] 機票

agreement [ə'grimənt] 協議；同意

suggest [sə'dʒɛst] 建議

quit [kwɪt] 終止

Unit 2. On vacation.

（休假）

實用例句

- I love the beach.
（我喜歡這海灘。）

- I am so glad we decided to vacation in Colorado.
（我很高興我們決定去科羅拉多州度假。）

- Let's extend our vacation another day.
（我們把假期多延一天吧。）

- Would you like to go sightseeing today?
（你今天要去到處逛逛嗎？）

- I enjoyed our vacation this year.
（我喜歡我們今年的假期。）

實用會話

A I am glad we chose a tropical place for our

vacation.
（我很高興我們選了到熱帶地區渡假。）

B Me, too.
（我也是。）

We can lie out in the sun all day.
（我們可以整天做陽光浴。）

A I am glad to be away from the winter weather in New York.
（我很高興可以躲開冬天的紐約。）

B I kind of miss home, though.
（但是我有些想家。）

A I don't. I don't want our vacation to end.
（我不會，我才不想結束休假呢。）

Let's stay a few more days.
（讓我們多待幾天吧！）

What do you say?
（你覺得呢？）

B **Great idea!**
（好主意。）

We can take a tour of the island.
（我們可以環島旅遊。）

A **Fantastic!**
（太棒了！）

I will call the tour agency.
（我來通知旅行社。）

B Okay.
（好的。）

But first, let's have lunch on the beach.
（但首先，我們先在海灘吃午餐吧。）

A That sounds like a great idea.
（這主意聽起來不錯。）

B We can talk about the tour while we eat.
（我們可以邊吃邊談。）

加強練習

➢ Great idea!

A: How about we go to the zoo on Saturday?

B: Great idea! I haven't been there in years.

A：週六去動物園逛逛如何？

B：太棒了！我好幾年沒去動物園了呢。

➢ Fantastic!

A: I got my first paycheck today.

B: Fantastic! Now you can go buy that new outfit you wanted.

A：我今天第一次拿到薪水。

B：太棒了！現在 你可以買你想要的新衣服了。

單字

beach [bitʃ] ⓝ 海濱

extend [ɪk'stɛnd]

sightsee ['saɪt'si] 觀光

tropical ['trɑpɪkḷ] 熱帶的

weather ['wɛðɚ] 天氣

miss [mɪs] ⓥ 想念

end [ɛnd] 結束

fantastic [fæn'tæstɪk] （口語）好極了；太美妙了

agency ['edʒənsɪ] ⓝ 代理商

zoo [zu] 動物園

Unit 3. Talking about the vacation

（玩回來後討論假期）

實用例句

- What was your favorite part of the trip?
（這趟旅遊你最喜歡那一部份？）

- Did you see the fabulous photos of Gary's trip to Greece?
（你有看過蓋瑞去希臘玩所拍的美麗照片嗎？）

- I can't wait to tell everyone about my vacation to Mexico.
（我等不及告訴大家我的墨西哥之行。）

- I hope I remember to tell Mom about the cute antique shop I went to in France.
（我希望能記得告訴我媽，有關法國那間古色古香的小店的事。）

- Bob told us that he saw a ghost while on his vacation in Spain.
（鮑伯告訴我們他去西班牙渡假時遇到了鬼。）

實用會話

A I am glad to be back home.
（我很高興回到家了。）

B I am, too.
（我也是。）

I enjoyed our trip, but there is no place like home.
（我喜歡這次的旅行，但還是家最好。）

A **Isn't that the truth!**
（那句話再真實也不過了。）

Still, I didn't really want to leave that beautiful mountain cabin though.
（但我仍然不願離開那間漂亮的山間小木屋。）

B I'm going to miss hiking in the woods.
（我會想念在山林中健行的經驗。）

A I'm going to miss the peaceful streams.
（我會想念寧靜的小溪流。）

B Now we are back in the city with all of its noise and stress.
（現在我們又回到充滿噪音與壓力的城市。）

A **That's okay.**
（還好啦。）

It's home.
（畢竟是家嘛。）

B I know.
（我知道。）

I wouldn't trade it for the world.
（拿全世界來換，我也不換。）

A But it is good to get away from time to time.
（但有時出去走一走也不錯。）

B That's true.
（說的也是。）

I look forward to our next trip to the country.
（我期待下次到鄉下去旅遊。）

加強練習

➢ Isn't that the truth!

A: I hate it when people talk loudly on the subway.

B: Isn't that the truth! That is totally disrespectful to others.

A：我討厭在地鐵談話喧嘩的人。

B：這倒是真的，那樣做對他人很不禮貌。

➢ That's okay.

A: Do you want to go to the store with us?

B: That's okay. I was planning to go later on.

A：你要與我們一起去商店嗎？

B：沒關係，我本來要晚一點才會去。

單字

favorite [ˈfevərɪt] 最喜歡的

part [pɑrt] 部份

fabulous [ˈfæbjələs] 極好的；絕妙的

photo [ˈfoto] 相片

remember [rɪˈmɛmbɚ] 記得

antique [ænˈtik] 古董

ghost [gost] 鬼

back [bæk] 回來

cabin [ˈkæbɪn] 小木屋

hiking [ˈhaɪkɪŋ] 健行；長途步行

miss [mɪs] ⓥ 想念

woods [wʊdz] 森林

stream [strim] ⓝ 小溪；流水

noise [nɔɪz] 雜音；噪音

stress [strɛs] 壓力

trade [tred] 貿易；交易

disrespectful [ˌdɪsrɪˈspɛktfəl] 沒禮貌

totally [ˈtotl̩ɪ] 完全的

Unit 4. Call in sick.

（請病假）

實用例句

- Josh called in sick today.
  （賈許打電話來請病假。）

- Ted calls in sick every other Friday.
  （泰德每兩星期的週五都會打電話請病假。）

- I can't call in sick. I used up all of my personal days.
  （我不能請病假，我已經把特休都用完了。）

- I am going to call in sick on Monday instead of using a vacation day.
  （我星期一打算請病假，而不用特休。）

- You should call in sick. You have a high fever.
  （你發高燒了，應該請病假。）

實用會話

A Have you seen Elsa?
（你有沒有看到愛沙？）

B She called in sick today.
（她今天請病假。）

A **Oh**. I hope she is feeling okay.
（喔，希望她快一點好起來。）

B Actually, she was sick yesterday, and she came in to work.
（事實上，她昨天就生病，但是仍然來上班。）

She felt worse and decided to go to the doctor.
（她覺得情況更嚴重了，所以決定去看醫生。）

A When is her doctor's appointment?
（她和醫師約什麼時候？）

B It was this morning.
（今天早上。）

The doctor ordered her to stay in bed for two days.
（醫師叮嚀她在家休息兩天。）

A **Wow.** I think I'll call her later to see how she's doing.
（哇，我想等一下打電話給她，看看她感覺如何。）

B That's a good idea. She is a good employee.
（好主意，她是個好員工。）

She never abuses her sick days.
（從不隨便請病假。）

A I know.
（我知道。）

When Elsa calls in sick, it is always something serious.
（當愛沙請假時，通常問題都很嚴重了。）

B We should send her a get-well card.
（我們應該寄張卡片給她，祝她早日康復。）

加強練習

➢ Oh.

A: Today, Bill came in to work 30 minutes late.
B: Oh. Yesterday, he was an hour late.

A：今天比爾上班遲到 30 分鐘。
B：喔，他昨天遲了 1 小時。

➢ Wow.

A: Did you know that Billy is back in town?
B: Wow. I haven't seen him in years.

A：你知道比爾已經回到城裏了嗎？

B：哇，我已經好幾年沒有見到他了。

單字

fever ['fivɚ] 發燒

worse [wɝs] 更糟的

decide [dɪ'saɪd] ⓥ 決定；判斷

appointment [ə'pɔɪntmənt] 約會；約定時間

order ['ɔrdɚ] ⓥ 命令

employee [,ɛmplɔɪ'ɪ] 雇員；員工

serious ['sɪrɪəs] 嚴重的

abuse [ə'bjuz] 濫用

Unit 5. Take some days off.

（休假幾天）

實用例句

• I have accumulated 5 days off so far this year.
（今年到現在我累積了 5 天假。）

• How many days off should I take?
（我應該休幾天假呢？）

• I am going to request 3 days off to relax.
（我將要休 3 天假，好好休息一下。）

• Billy took 2 days off to go visit his girlfriend.
（比利休假兩天去看他女朋友。）

• Jessica is planning to take 4 days off to study for her college entrance exam.
（傑西卡計劃要休假 4 天，準備大學入學考試 。）

實用會話

A I have been working 50 hours a week for the

past month.
（過去整個月，我每週都工作 50 小時。）

B **Really?**
（真的嗎？）

You should take some days off.
（你應該要休息幾天。）

A I can't. I have to meet the project deadline.
（不行，我必須要截止日前把案子做好。）

B I think the boss will understand.
（我想老板會體諒的。）

You will be more effective if you take some time off.
（如果你休息，辦事會更有效率。）

A **That's true.**
（這倒是真的。）

Maybe I will request 2 days off next week.
（也許我下週該請假 2 天。）

I will have to postpone the project deadline three days if I take time off, though.
（如果我休假的話，案子的截止日就得往後延三天。）

B It's okay.
（還好啦。）

I think everyone will understand.
（我想大家都會體諒的。）

You are a hard worker and deserve a break.
（你工作很努力，應該休息一下。）

A Thanks.
（謝謝。）

I will make a formal request tomorrow.
（我明天將正式提出假單。）

B You will be glad you did.
（你這樣做是對的。）

A Do you have any suggestions for my days off?
（這幾天休假，你建議我去哪裡走走呢？）

B You should visit a spa and get a relaxation treatment.
（你可以去泡 spa 作緩壓水療。）

加強練習

➢ Really?

A: I have to cancel our dinner plans.

B: Really? I am sorry to hear that.

A：我必須取消我們的晚餐計劃。

B：真的嗎？太可惜了。

➢ That's true.

A: We should keep our relationship professional since we are co-workers.

B: That's true. I am sorry for asking you out on a date.

A：既然我們是同事，就應該維持專業的關係。

B：這倒是真的，我不應該約你出去的。

單字

accumulate [ə'kjumjə,let] 累積

request [rɪ'kwɛst] 要求

relax [rɪ'læks] 放輕鬆

past [pæst] ⓐ過去的

really ['riəlɪ] 真的

project ['prɑdʒɛkt] 專案；企畫；學校研究作業

deadline ['dɛd,laɪn] 截止日期

boss [bɔs] ⓝ 主管；老闆

understand [,ʌndɚ'stænd] 瞭解；明白

effective [ɪ'fɛktɪv] ⓐ 有效的

postpone [post'pon] ⓥ 延期

deserve [dɪ'zɝv] ⓥ 應得的；得之無愧的

break [brek] ⓝ短暫的休息

formal ['fɔrml̩] ⓐ 正式的

suggestion [sə'dʒɛstʃən] 建議

relaxation [rɪlæks'eʃən] 休息；放輕鬆

treatment ['tritmənt] 處理

cancel ['kænsl̩] ⓥ 取消；中止

relationship [rɪ'leʃən,ʃɪp] 關係

professional [prə'fɛʃənl̩] 專業的

CHAPTER 5

SOCIAL ACTIVITY
社交活動

Unit 1. Birthday Party

生日派對

實用例句

- Are you going to Jonathan's birthday party?
（你要去強納生的生日派對嗎？）

- I am going to get Mandy a Barbie doll for her birthday.
（我打算要去買芭比娃娃給嫚蒂當作生日禮物。）

- When is Ted's birthday party?
（泰德的生日派對是什麼時候？）

- I hope John doesn't find out about his surprise birthday party.
（我希望約翰不會發現他的驚喜生日派對。）

- Can you help me decorate for Pam's birthday party?
（你可以幫我佈置潘的生日派對嗎？）

實用會話

A Timmy's birthday party is next week.

（提米的生日派對是下禮拜。）

Will you be able to come?

（你能參加嗎？）

B I don't know.

（我不確定。）

I am working late all next week.

（我下週整個星期都會工作到很晚。）

A What time are you getting off work?

（你幾點下班？）

B I am leaving at 10:00 pm

（我十點下班。）

Will that be too late?

（那會太晚嗎？）

A Well, the party starts at 8:00 p.m, but it will still be going on at 10:00 p.m.

（慶生會八點開始，但十點鐘時應該還持續著。）

B **Wonderful.**

（太好了。）

I will rush home from work and try to be at the party by 11:00 pm.
（下班後我會盡快趕回家，試著在十一點以前趕到慶生會。）

A You may miss the cake and punch.
（你可能會錯過蛋糕和水果酒。）

B **That's okay**.
（沒關係。）

At least I will still be able to give Timmy his gift.
（至少我可以把要給提米的禮物給他。）

A I will put you in the guest list then.
（那我就把你列在賓客名單上了。）

B Thanks a lot.
（謝啦！）

I will see you next week.
（下週見。）

加強練習

➢ Wonderful

A: Carmen is getting her braces off today.

B: Wonderful. I can't wait to see her beautiful new smile.

A：卡門今天要拆掉牙齒矯正器。

B：太好了，我等不及要看她美麗的笑容。

➢ That's okay

A: Can I help you shine your shoes?

B: That's okay. I am almost finished.

A：需要我幫你擦鞋子嗎？

B： 沒關係，我幾乎快好了。

單字

birthday [ˈbɝθˌde] ⓝ 生日

surprise [sɚˈpraɪz] 驚奇；驚喜

decorate [ˈdɛkəˌret] 裝飾

late [let] 很晚

wonderful [ˈwʌndɚfəl] 好棒的；絕妙的；好極了

rush [rʌʃ] 急著趕

gift [gɪft] 禮物

guest list 賓客名單

brace [bres] 牙齒矯正器

smile [smaɪl] 笑容

shine [ʃaɪn] 擦亮（皮鞋）

almost [ˈɔlˌmost] ⓐⓓⓥ 幾乎

Unit 2. Wedding

（婚禮）

實用例句

- My sister's wedding is on Valentine's Day.
  （我姐姐的婚禮在情人節那天。）
- When is Tim's wedding?
  （提姆的婚禮是什麼時候？）
- I can't wait until my wedding day!
  （我無法等到自己結婚的那天了。）
- I always cry at weddings.
  （在婚禮中，我總會掉眼淚。）
- Judy is a hostess at Ann's wedding.
  （茱蒂將在安妮的婚禮中擔任女招待。）

實用會話

A Hurry!

（快一點！）

We are going to be late for Molly's wedding.
（我們快趕不上茉莉的婚禮了。）

B **Gosh!**
（天啊！）

I am going as fast as I can.
（我已經儘可能地快了。）

A Well, move faster!
（那就再快一點！）

We have to be there in an hour!
（我們必須在一個小時內趕到。）

B I will be finished in ten minutes.
（我十分鐘內可以做好。）

Quit rushing me.
（不要再催我了。）

A **For goodness sake!**
（拜託！）

It takes an hour just to drive there.
（光開車到那兒，就要花上一個鐘頭。）

B Really?
（真的嗎？）

I though it was faster than that.
（我以為會少於一個鐘頭。）

A Nope.

（不是。）

That is why we must hurry.

（所以我們才得要快一點。）

B I understand.

（我瞭解了。）

I'll try to hurry.

（我會試著快一點。）

A As long as we leave soon, I think we'll be ok.

（只要我們趕快出發，應該就不會有問題。）

Weddings hardly ever begin on time.

（婚禮很少準時。）

I hope Molly is also running late.

（我希望茉莉也會遲到。）

B So do I.

（我也是。）

加強練習

➢ Gosh!

A: Gosh! Look at how fast that dog is running!

B: I know. He must be chasing something.

A：天啊！看看那隻狗跑的多快。

B： 我看到了，牠一定是在追什麼東西。

➢ For goodness sake!

A: Hurry up and finish you dinner.

B: For goodness sake! I just sat down to eat 2 minutes ago!

A：快點吃完你的晚餐。

B： 拜託！我兩分鐘前才剛剛坐下呢。

單字

wedding [ˈwɛdɪŋ] 婚禮

cry [kraɪ] 哭

hostess [ˈhostɪs] 女主人

sake [sek] ⓝ 緣故；理由

hurry [ˈhɝɪ] 匆忙；趕快

leave [liv] 離開

hardly [ˈhɑrdlɪ] 幾乎不

chase [tʃes] 追逐

finish [ˈfɪnɪʃ] 完成

Unit 3. Christmas Party

聖誕晚會

實用例句

- Does your office throw an annual Christmas party?
（你們公司每年有舉辦聖誕晚會嗎？）

- What are you taking to the Christmas party?
（你們都帶什麼去參加聖誕晚會？）

- I hate going to Christmas parties.
（我討厭參加聖誕晚會。）

- Will you please bring the eggnog for the Christmas party?
（聖誕晚會你可以帶蛋酒來嗎？）

- Will there be dancing at the school Christmas party?
（學校的聖誕晚會中可以跳舞嗎？）

實用會話

A Would you be my date for the office Christmas party?

（我們公司的聖誕晚會，你可以當我的舞伴嗎？）

B I'd love to, but Jim already asked me.

（我很願意，但吉姆已經約我了。）

A **That's cool.**

（那不錯啊。）

I guess I will go alone.

（我想我只好一個人去了。）

B Do you know Trisha?

（你認識泰瑞莎嗎？）

She needs a date.

（她需要一個舞伴。）

A I've only spoken to her a few times.

（我只跟她說過幾次話。）

She may not want to go with me.

（她也許不會想跟我一起去。）

B She mentioned that she was hoping you would ask her.

（她曾提過希望你能開口約她。）

She has a crush on you.

（她蠻喜歡你的。）

A **Wow!** I never knew.

（哇！我從來都不知道。）

B It's true.

（是真的。）

A Maybe I will give her a call tonight and ask her to the party.

（也許我今天晚上會打個電話給她，邀請她一起去舞會。）

B Sounds good. I think she'll be thrilled.

（聽起來不錯，我想她會很高興的。）

加強練習

➢ That's cool.

A: Matt went bungee jumping last night.

B: That's cool. I wish I were brave enough to go bungee jumping!

A：馬特昨晚去高空彈跳。

B：太棒了，我希望我也有足夠的勇氣去參加高空彈跳。

➢ Wow!

A: The police finally caught the serial killer.

B: Wow! I will feel safer now that he's been put in jail.

A：警察終於抓到那個連續殺人犯。

B：哇！他被關起來後，現在我可以放心了。

單字

annual [ˈænjʊəl] 每年的

date [det] 舞伴

mention [ˈmɛnʃən] 提起；談及

crush [krʌʃ]（口語）熱戀

thrilled [ˈθrɪld] 非常興奮（thrill 的過去分詞）

brave [brev] 勇敢的

serial [ˈsɪrɪəl] 連續的

killer [ˈkɪlɚ] ⓝ 殺手

jail [dʒel] ⓝ 監獄

caught [kɔt] ⓥ 捕捉

finally [ˈfaɪnl̩ɪ] 最終；終於

Unit

4. Farewell Party

（送別會）

實用例句

- When is Peter's going away party?
（彼得的送別會是什麼時候？）

- I am sad that Tom is leaving, but at least I will see him one last time at the farewell party.
（湯姆要離開，我很離過，但至少我在告別聚會時，可以再見他一次。）

- I am throwing Mike a farewell party, and you are invited.
（我要幫麥克舉辦一個送別會，你可要來哦。）

- Has anyone seen the guest list for Kim's farewell party?
（有任何人看到金的送別會賓客名單嗎？）

- I can't go to George's going away party; I have a cold.
（我感冒了，所以無法參加喬治的送別會。）

實用會話

A Jake is leaving town for good.
（傑克要離開了。）

He got a job out-of-state, so we're throwing him a farewell party.
（他在別州找到工作，所以我們要替他舉辦一個送別會。）

B **How exciting!**
（好棒哦！）

I knew he had been looking for a career change.
（我知道他一直希望能夠變換職業跑道。）

When is the party?
（送別會是什麼時候？）

A The party is a week from today.
（送別會是下個禮拜的今天。）

Will you be able to attend?
（你會參加嗎？）

B **Of course!**
（當然！）

I wouldn't miss this party for the world!
（我絕對不會錯過這個聚會。）

A Jake is a good person.
（傑克是個好人。）

I am glad that he gets this chance at a better life.
（我很高興他有這個機會，可以過更好的生活。）

B Me, too.
（我也是。）

But I am sad that he is leaving.
（但他要離開，我很難過。）

At least we can have a nice party one last time to let him know how much we care about him.
（至少我們可以辦一次美好的聚會，讓他知道我們有多在乎他。）

A That's true.
（這倒是真的。）

Will you be able to bring something?
（你可以帶些東西來嗎？）

B I can buy something from the store.
（我可以去店裡買些東西。）

A That's fine.
（好。）

Anything will do.
（買什麼都可以。）

B I will bring a salad.

（我會帶沙拉。）

加強練習

➢ How exciting!

A: I am going to New York for summer vacation.

B: How exciting! New York is filled with fun things to do.

A：我要去紐約度暑假。

B：真是令人興奮！紐約有很多好玩的事情可以做。

➢ Of course!

A: Could you please cook dinner tonight?

B: Of course! I love to cook.

A：今晚你可以準備晚餐嗎？

B：當然，我很喜歡做菜。

單字

farewell [fɛr′wɛl] 告別

invite [ɪn′vaɪt] 邀請

cold [kold] ⓝ 感冒

career [kə'rɪr] ⓝ生涯規劃；事業

attend [ə'tɛnd] ⓥ 參加；出席

exciting [ɪk'saɪtɪŋ] 令人興奮的

cook [kʊk] ⓥ 烹調；煮

Unit 5. Go to see the fireworks

（去看煙火）

實用例句

- Let's go see the fireworks.
（我們去看煙火吧！）

- Kim loves watching fireworks on Fourth of July.
（金很喜歡在七月四號去看煙火。）

- Fireworks are illegal within the city limits. Let's drive to the country and see them.
（在都市範圍內放煙火是不合法的，我們開車到鄉下去看吧。）

- Can Mike watch fireworks with us?
（麥可能不能跟我們一起去看煙火？）

- We're having a fireworks-watching party. Would you like to come?
（我們要辦一個煙火觀賞派對，你們想來嗎？）

實用會話

A Do you like going to see fireworks?

（你們喜歡去看煙火嗎？）

B They are okay. I would rather watch them on T.V. though.

（還好。我比較喜歡看電視上的。）

A Oh, well, Sally has invited us to go see the fireworks display downtown.

（喔， 好吧，莎麗邀請我們去看市中心的煙火表演。）

B **Is that so?** Well, I am going to pass.

（是這樣嗎？好吧，那我就不去了。）

I will just watch them on T.V.

（我看電視上的就好了。）

A It is a lot better to see them up close in person.

（親眼去看放煙火將是更棒的經驗。）

B I don't feel like going out this late at night.

（我不想這麼晚出去。）

A I understand.

（我瞭解。）

I will let Sally know.

（我會告知莎麗的。）

B **Thanks.**

（謝啦！）

I think I might actually just go to bed early.

（事實上，我想我可能會早點睡覺。）

A What about the fireworks?

（那煙火表演呢？）

B I will record the news tonight and watch them on T.V. tomorrow.

（我會把今晚的夜間新聞錄下來，明天再放來看。）

加強練習

➢ Is that so?

A: Julie broke her leg yesterday.

B: Is that so? I heard she sprained her ankle.

A：茱麗昨天摔斷了腿。

B：是嗎？我聽說她扭傷了腳踝。

➢ Thanks.

A: I will give Suzy the message.

B: Thanks. I hope she understands.

A：我會把這個訊息告知蘇茜的。

B：謝啦。我希望她能瞭解。

單字

firework [ˈfaɪrwɝk] 煙火

illegal [ɪˈlig!] ⓐ 不法的；非法

limit [ˈlɪmɪt] ⓝ 界限；範圍

country [ˈkʌntrɪ] ⓝ鄉下

display [dɪsˈple] 展示；陳列

downtown [ˈdaʊnˈtaʊn] 市區；市中心

pass [pæs] 不參加

record [rɪˈkɔrd] ⓥ 錄影

sprain [spren] 扭傷

ankle [ˈæŋk!] 腳踝

message [ˈmɛsɪdʒ] 留言；訊息

Unit 6. Go on picnics

（去野餐）

實用例句

- What should I bring to tomorrow's picnic?
（明天野餐我該帶些什麼？）

- Are you going camping this weekend?
（你這個週末要去露營嗎？）

- I don't like camping because of all of the insects.
（我不喜歡露營，因為會碰到很多種類的昆蟲。）

- Today is great weather for a picnic.
（今天是個野餐的好天氣。）

- I would like for you to come to our monthly picnic next week.
（我想邀請你下週來參加我們每月舉辦的野餐。）

實用會話

A Today is a great day for a picnic.
（今天是個野餐的好日子。）

B I know. The weather is nice and warm.
（我知道，因為天氣又好又　　。）

A Let's have a picnic lunch in the park.
（一起去在公園野餐吧！）

B That's a great idea.
（那是個好主意。）

What should we take?
（我們該帶什麼呢？）

A We can take sandwiches, chips, and soda.
（我們可以帶些三明治、餅乾和沙拉。）

But what should we take for dessert?
（但甜點要帶些什麼呢？）

B How about watermelon?
（帶西瓜怎麼樣？）

A **Awesome.**
（太好了！）

This will be a nice picnic.
（這將是個美好的野餐。）

B We can also take our bikes and ride along the trail.
（我們也可以帶腳踏車延著路騎。）

A **Fantastic!**
（太棒了！）

We can get some much-needed exercise.
（我們可以得到我們欠缺的運動量。）

B This is going to be so much fun!
（這一定會很好玩的。）

加強練習

➢ Awesome

A: Julie and Jamie both made the swim team.
B: Awesome! They both deserved to make it.

A：茱麗和潔咪都加入了游泳校隊。
B：太好了！那是她們應得的。

➢ Fantastic

A: I made reservations for us at the Olive Garden.
B: Fantastic. I have been craving pasta all week.

A：我在橄欖花園訂了位。

B：太棒了！我想吃義大利麵已經想了一整個禮拜了。

單字

picnic [ˈpɪknɪk] 野餐

insect [ˈɪnsɛkt] ⓝ 昆蟲

camp [kæmp] ⓝ 營區；ⓥ 露營

monthly [ˈmʌnθlɪ] 每月的

park [pɑrk] 公園

dessert [dɪˈzɝt] ⓝ 飯後）甜點

awesome [ˈɔsəm]（口語）很棒的

trail [trel] 路徑

fantastic [fænˈtæstɪk]（口語）好極了；太美妙了

exercise [ˈɛksɚˌsaɪz] 運動

reservation [ˌrɛzɚˈveʃən] 預訂

CHAPTER 6

HOBBY/SPORTS

嗜好和運動

Unit 1. Playing basketball
（打籃球）

實用例句

- I play basketball for an hour every day for exercise.
（我每天打籃球一個小時當作運動。）

- How long have you been playing basketball?
（你籃球打了多久？）

- I made the school varsity basketball team.
（我參加了大學校際籃球隊。）

- Let's go to the park and play basketball.
（我們一起去公園打籃球吧！）

- Molly, would you like to join our basketball club?
（茉莉，妳想加入我們籃球俱樂部嗎？）

實用會話

A Hey, did Jamie ever make it to the basketball game?
（嗨，傑咪有機會打籃球嗎？）

B No, she had to go in to work early.
（不，她必須很早上班。）

A **How awful!**
（這真是太糟了！）

They are always making her go in to work early.
（他們總是叫她很早去上班。）

B We just played a second game later on that night when she got off work.
（當她晚上下班後，我們才進行第二場賽。）

It was a lot of fun.
（真的很好玩。）

You should play with us next time.
（下次，你應該跟我們一起打。）

A Sure! That sounds like fun.
（當然，聽起來很有意思。）

When are you guys getting together again for a game?
（你們下次碰面玩球是什麼時候？）

B We will probably meet on Sunday afternoon.
（可能是星期天下午吧。）

A That would be a great time for me.
（這時間對我來說剛好。）

B **Terrific.**
（太好了！）

We are planning to play for a couple of hours.
（我們計畫要打好幾個鐘頭。）

A Okay. I will bring plenty of water.
（好，我會帶足夠的水來。）

B You'll need it.
（你會需要的。）

We plan to work up a sweat.
（我們計畫要流很多汗。）

加強練習

➢ How awful!

A: Jane slipped and fell in the mud today.

B: How awful! Is she hurt?

A：今天珍滑倒在泥巴裡。

B：真糟糕，她有受傷嗎？

➢ Terrific.

A: I am getting married!

B: Terrific! When did he propose?

A：我要結婚了。

B：太棒了！他什麼時候求婚的？

單字

exercise [ˈɛksɚˌsaɪz] 運動

basketball [ˈbæskɪtˌbɔl] ⓝ 籃球

team [tim] 隊伍；團隊

join [dʒɔɪn] 加入

fun [fʌn] 好玩；樂趣

terrific [təˈrɪfɪk] 很好的

sweat [swɛt] 流汗

mud [mʌd] 泥巴

hurt [hɝt] 痛；傷害

propose [prəˈpoz] 求婚

Unit 2.

Playing soccer

（踢足球）

實用例句

- Soccer is a difficult sport.
（足球是一個困難的運動。）

- Peter plays soccer three times a week.
（彼得一週踢三次足球。）

- I am dedicated to increasing my skill as a soccer player.
（我認真要改善自己身為足球員的技巧。）

- Does Jan play soccer?
（珍踢足球嗎？）

- I am trying out for the city soccer league.
（我想試著加入都會足球聯盟。）

實用會話

A I am going to a soccer game today.

（今天我要去看足球賽。）

B Really?

（真的？）

Could I go too?

（我可以一起去嗎？）

A Well, I already bought my ticket.

（可是我已經買好票了。）

You might be able to buy a ticket at the gate.

（你可能可以在入口處買門票。）

B Would I be able to sit with you?

（我會和你坐在一起嗎？）

A Yes. It is general admission.

（可以，那是不劃位的票。）

B **Great.**

（太好了！）

I will call the ticket office to see if they are still selling tickets.

（我會打電話去售票辦公室，問是否仍有售票。）

I love soccer.

（我熱愛足球。）

A I do, too.

（我也是。）

I have been playing since I was five.
（我從五歲大時就開始玩足球。）

B I don't play, but I love to watch.
（我不玩足球，但喜歡看足球賽。）

A It's a great sport.
（那是個很棒的運動。）

There is a lot of skill involved.
（需要許多技巧。）

B **I know.**
（我知道。）

That's why I appreciate the game so much.
（這是為什麼我很喜歡觀賞球賽的原因。）

加強練習

➢ Great

A: I reached my weight loss goal.

B: Great. I knew you could do it.

A：我達到減重目標了。

B：太好了，我就知道你辦得到。

➢ I know

A: Maria won't be in for work today.

B: I know. She called me and left a message.

A：瑪麗亞今天不會來上班。

B：我知道，她有打電話留言給我。

單字

difficult [ˈdɪfəˌkʌlt] ⓐ 困難的

soccer [ˈsɑkɚ] 足球

dedicated [ˈdɛdɪˌketɪd] 一心一意的；專注的；很投入的

increase [ɪnˈkris] 增加；增強

skill [skɪl] 技巧

league [lig] 聯盟

general [ˈdʒɛnərəl] 一般的

admission [ədˈmɪʃən] ⓝ 准予入場

involve [ɪnˈvɑlv] 牽涉

appreciate [əˈpriʃɪˌet] ⓥ 鑑賞；感激

goal [gol] 目標

Unit

3. Collecting coins

（收集硬幣）

實用例句

- I have been collecting coins for 10 years.
（我已經收集硬幣十年了。）

- Todd has coins from all over the world.
（陶德有全世界各地方的硬幣。）

- Travis is starting a coin-collecting club.
（崔維斯將要成立一個硬幣收集俱樂部。）

- I have over 100 coins in my collection.
（我的硬幣收藏超過一百。）

- Could you help me start my own coin collection?
（你可以幫我開始我個人的硬幣收集嗎？）

實用會話

A James went to the coin collecting convention.

（詹姆士去硬幣收集大會了。）

B How long has he been collecting coins?
（他收集硬幣多久了？）

A He has been a collector for about 15 years.
（他是十五年的收藏家了。）

B **How interesting!**
（好有趣喔！）

Do you know what made him start that hobby?
（你知道是什麼原因，讓他開始這個興趣的嗎？）

A I believe his father got him interested in it.
（我想是他爸爸讓他產生興趣的。）

His dad owns a coin shop.
（他爸爸有一間硬幣店。）

B Wow! What an interesting hobby.
（哇！好有趣的嗜好！）

I should ask him if some of my old coins are worth anything.
（我應該問他，看看我的一些舊硬幣是否有價值。）

A You should do that.
（你應該那樣做。）

He is pretty accurate at valuing old coins.
（他對於舊硬幣的價值很有概念。）

B Do you know how much his collection is worth?

（你知道他的收藏有多少價值？）

A His collection is valued at $100,000.

（他的收集值十萬美金。）

B **Oh, my!** That's impressive.

（天啊！真是讓人印象深刻。）

加強練習

➢ How interesting!

A: On the field trip, we looked at fossils!

B: How interesting! I wish I could have gone, too.

A：在這次旅行中，我們觀賞了化石。

B：好有趣！ 真希望我也有去。

➢ Oh, my!

A: Oh, my! That little girl just tripped and fell over.

B: Oh, no! I hope she's ok.

A：天啊！那個小女孩被絆了一下、跌倒了。

B：喔！不！ 希望她沒事。

單字

collect [kə'lɛkt] ⓥ 收集

coin [kɔɪn] 硬幣

collection [kə'lɛkʃən] 精品系列；收藏品

convention [kən'vɛnʃən] 集會

hobby ['hɑbɪ] 嗜好

own [on] ⓝ擁有

accurate ['ækjə,rɪt] 準確的

value ['vælju] ⓥ 估價

worth [wɝθ] 價值

impressive [ɪm'prɛsɪv] 印象深刻的

fossil ['fɑsḷ] 化石

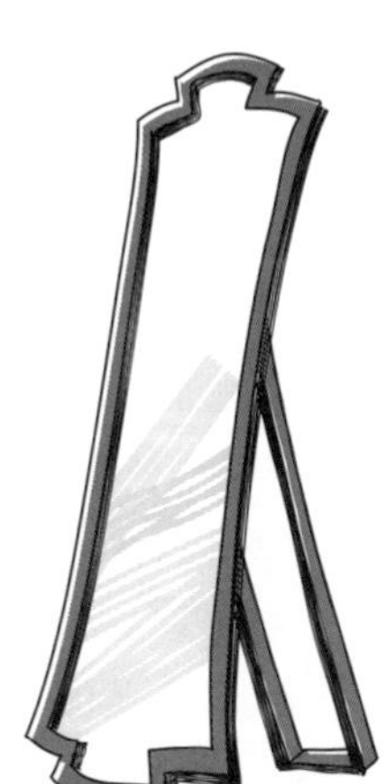

Unit 4. Playing the piano

（彈鋼琴）

實用例句

• How long does it take to be a great pianist?
（成為一個成功的鋼琴家要花多久時間？）

• I practice piano every day for two hours.
（我每天練二小時鋼琴。）

• Stella has been playing the piano since she was three years old.
（史黛拉從三歲就開始彈鋼琴了。）

• I started taking piano lessons last month.
（上個月我開始上鋼琴課。）

• Can you show me how to play the piano?
（你可以告訴我如何彈鋼琴嗎？）

實用會話

A I get tired of practicing the piano.

（我對於練鋼琴感到厭煩。）

B But you are such a good pianist.

（但你是很棒的鋼琴家啊。）

A I have to practice 2 hours a day.

（我必須每天練習二小時。）

B You will appreciate it later on.

（將來你會感謝這種練習的。）

A You're probably right.

（你也許是對的。）

Sometimes I just wish I could do other things instead of practice.

（有時候我只希望可以做做其他的事，而不只是一直練習。）

B I understand. When you get older, you can still have piano as a hobby.

（我瞭解。當你再年長一些，你仍可以把鋼琴當作嗜好。）

A **That's true.**

（那倒是真的。）

I guess I will suffer through practice until I can appreciate playing more.

（我想我會繼續忍耐，直到自己可以領悟演奏的樂趣。）

B **Good choice.**

（好選擇！）

Maybe you could practice in thirty-minute intervals instead of two-hour intervals.
（也許你可以每次練習半小時，而不是一次練習兩小時。）

A That's a great idea.
（那是個好主意。）

That would make it easier for me to deal with.
（這樣對我來説容易多了。）

B Well, good luck with your practicing.
（好吧！祝你練習順利。）

加強練習

➢ That's true.

A: Billy should focus more on schoolwork.

B: That's true. I rarely see him study.

A：比利應該多專注在學校課程上。

B：這倒是真的，我很少看到他在念書。

➢ Good choice.

A: I think I will take a music appreciation class next semester.

B: Good choice. I learned a lot when I took that class.

A：我想我下學期會上一門音樂欣賞課程。

B：好選擇。當我在上那門課時，學到很多東西。

單字

pianist [pɪˈænɪst] 鋼琴家

practice [ˈpræktɪs] 練習

probably [ˈprɑbəblɪ] 或許；可能的

suffer [ˈsʌfɚ] ⓥ 遭難；受苦

interval [ˈɪntɚvl̩] 間隔

rarely [ˈrɛrlɪ] 不常；難得的

focus [ˈfokəs] 專注

appreciation [əpriʃɪˈeʃən] 欣賞

Unit 5.

Playing volleyball

（玩排球）

實用例句

- Jenny is a great volleyball player.
  （珍妮是一個優秀的排球員。）

- Would you like to go to the beach and play a game of volleyball?
  （你想要去海邊，玩沙灘排球嗎？）

- I have been playing volleyball for years.
  （我玩排球已經好多年了。）

- Volleyball is a great way to stay in shape.
  （玩排球是一個保持身材的好方法。）

- Playing volleyball helps develop hand-eye coordination.
  （玩排球幫助人們發展手眼協調能力。）

實用會話

A Volleyball is not my best sport, but I really enjoy playing it.
（排球不是我最擅長的運動，但我真的很喜歡打排球。）

B Yeah. It's a good way to get exercise.
（是啊，那是個好的運動方式。）

A Well, it builds hand-eye coordination, but I don't see how you get that much exercise.
（是的，它培養手眼協調能力，但我看不出來打排球可以有那麼多的運動量。）

There isn't a lot of running or moving involved.
（打排球不用大幅度的跑步或移動。）

B That's true. But it takes speed to run and hit the ball over the net.
（那倒是真的，但打排球需要跑的很快，把球打過中線。）

All of that running can give you quite a workout.
（這些跑步都可帶給你相當的運動。）

A In all of my years of playing volleyball, I find that it doesn't really give me a good workout.
（在我打排球的這些年，我發現它沒有真正讓我運動到。）

B Well, let's agree to disagree.
（好吧，該我們同意各人可以有不同的意見吧。）

A Sounds good.
（聽起來不錯！）

Do you want to meet up to play one day?
（想找一天一起打球嗎？）

B **Sure.**
（好啊。）

How about we play at the beach this weekend?
（這個週末去海邊玩排球如何？）

A Sounds like a plan.
（聽起來是個不錯的計劃。）

B **Great.**
（太好了。）

I'll see you in a few days.
（過兩天見了。）

加強練習

➢ Sure.

A: Could you give me a ride to the post office?

B: Sure. I can take you in a little while.

A：你可以順道載我一程去郵局嗎？

B：當然，再等我一下就可以帶你去。

➢ Great.

A: I am coming to town for a visit next month.

B: Great. We will have to meet up for dinner.

A：我下個月要到城裡拜訪。

B：太好了，我們可以碰面吃個晚飯。

單字

volleyball [ˈvɑlɪbɔl] 排球

shape [ʃep] 形狀

develop [dɪˈvɛləp] 發展

coordination [koɔrdṇˈeʃən] 協調

speed [spid] 速度

net [nɛt] 球網

disagree [ˌdɪsəˈgri] ⓥ 意見不合；不同意

CHAPTER 7

RESERVATION

預訂

Unit 1. Book a hotel room

（預訂旅館房間）

實用例句

- How many rooms would you like to reserve?
（你想預訂幾間房？）

- Do you have hotel reservations?
（你有預訂旅館房間嗎？）

- I forgot to book a hotel room for our vacation!
（我忘記為我們的假期預訂旅館房間。）

- Remind Jan to reserve 3 rooms for next week.
（提醒珍為下星期預訂三個房間。）

- I called the travel agent and asked her to book us a hotel.
（我打電話給旅行社服務人員，請她幫我們訂旅館。）

實用會話

A I need to reserve hotel rooms for the annual

convention taking place next month.
（為了下個月要召開的年度會議，我需要預訂旅館房間。）

B How many do you think we will need?
（你認為我們需要幾個房間？）

A I am assuming we will need at least 10 rooms.
（我想至少要 10 間。）

B Oh, no! That will cost a lot of money.
（哇，那得花很多錢呢。）

How many people are going?
（有多少人要去？）

A 20 people have signed up.
（有 20 個人登記了。）

We will be sleeping two to a room.
（我們會安排 2 個人睡一間房。）

B I think you should reserve 5 rooms.
（那麼你需要 5 個房間。）

A hotel room can have up to four occupants.
（旅館房間一間最多可以睡 4 個人。）

A **Is that so?**
（是嗎？）

I thought the maximum was two to a room.
（我以為一間最多 2 個人。）

B No.
（不。）

You can definitely sleep 4 to a room.
（你絕對可以安排 4 個人睡一間房。）

A Okay.
（好吧。）

I will call the Holiday Inn and book 5 rooms.
（我會打電話給假日飯店訂 5 間房。）

B Sounds good to me.
（聽起來很好。）

加強練習

➢ Oh, no!

A: I drank too much coffee.

B: Oh, no! I hope you won't be too jittery.

A：我喝了太多咖啡。

B：天啊，我希望你不會太過亢奮。

➢ Is that so?

A: I can't keep up in history class?

B: Is that so? It'd probably help if you stopped falling asleep during lecture.

A：我歷史課的進度趕不上。

B：這樣啊。如果你上課不再打瞌睡，情況可能會好一點。

單字

reserve [rɪ'zɝv] 預訂

reservation [ˌrɛzə'veʃən] 預訂

vacation [və'keʃən] ⓝ 休假；假期

forgot [fə'gɑt] 忘記（forget 的過去式）

book [bʊk] ⓥ 預訂

agent ['edʒənt] 代理人

annual ['ænjuəl] 每年的

assume [ə'sjum] 假定；臆測

occupant ['ɑkjəpənt] 居住者

maximum ['mæksɪməm] 最多

definitely ['dɛfənətlɪ] 確定地；肯定地

jittery ['dʒɪtərɪ] 緊張不安的

lecture ['lɛktʃə] 演講；講課

Unit

2. Book a flight

（訂機票）

實用例句

- What airline do you want to use to book our next flight?
（我們下一次飛行，你想要搭哪一家的飛機？）

- Call the travel agent and check to see if our flight has been booked.
（打電話給旅行社，查一查我們的班機是否已經預訂好了。）

- How many tickets do I need to book for the trip to Florida?
（我應該為佛羅里達之行訂幾張機票？）

- I don't know how to use the online flight ticket service.
（我不知道怎麼用線上機票預約系統。）

- I was on hold for an hour trying to book our flight.
（為了要訂我們的機票，我在電話上等了一個小時。）

實用會話

A Did Janice make it to Florida?
（珍妮絲去佛羅里達了嗎？）

B Yes, but barely.
（去了，但差點去不成。）

She forgot to book her flight.
（她忘了訂機票。）

A **Oh, my!** What did she do?
（天啊，那她後來怎麼辦？）

B She went to the airport and got on the waiting list.
（她去機場排候補。）

Luckily, there was a cancellation at the last minute.
（還好有人在最後一刻取消其行程。）

A Was she able to get that person's spot?
（她拿到那個人的位置了嗎？）

B Yes, but it cost her twice as much money for the ticket.
（有，但她花了 2 倍的錢。）

A **How dreadful!**
（多令人不快啊。）

That is an expensive lesson to learn.
（這個教訓的代價真昂貴。）

B Yes, but I bet she won't forget to book a flight in advance from now on.
（是的，我敢打賭她從今以後不會再忘記要先訂機票了。）

A That's true.
（這倒是真的。）

I hope this incident doesn't spoil her trip.
（我希望這件事不會影響她這趟旅行。）

B I spoke with her today.
（我今天和她通過話。）

She seems to be having a fun time despite the flight arrangements.
（她似乎玩得很愉快，雖然機票安排出了點問題。）

加強練習

➢ Oh, my!

A: There is a wild pig running down the street.

B: Oh, my! We should call the animal control agency.

A：有一隻野豬在街上亂跑。

B：天啊，我們應該打電話給動物控制管理當局。

➢ How dreadful!

A: Molly was in a car accident.

B: How dreadful! Will she be all right?

A：茉莉出了車禍。

B：那真糟糕，她還好嗎？

單字

flight [flaɪt] 飛行；班機

barely [ˈbɛrlɪ] adv 幾乎不能

airport [ˈɛrˌport] n 飛機場

cancellation [kæsəˈleʃən] n 取消

dreadful [ˈdrɛdfəl] 可怕的；（口語）糟透的

advance [ədˈvæns] n 預先

bet [bɛt] v 打賭

spoil [spɔɪl] 寵壞

incident [ˈɪnsədn̩t] n 意外事件；偶發事件

despite [dɪˈspaɪt] 儘管

arrangement [əˈrendʒmənt] 安排

control [kənˈtrol] 控制

Unit 3.

Reserve a table

（預約餐廳桌位）

實用例句

- I made dinner reservations at Chez Gerard for next Saturday night.
  （我預訂了下週六晚上到 Chez Gerard 餐廳用餐。）

- Did you reserve a table for Dad's surprise birthday party?
  （你有為爸爸的驚喜派對訂席嗎？）

- How many tables should Jim reserve for the office party?
  （吉米應該為公司的派對預約幾桌？）

- Jenny forgot to reserve a table for dinner tonight.
  （珍妮忘記為今晚的晚餐預訂位置了。）

- Who do I call to cancel a reservation I no longer need?
  （我預訂的桌位不需要了，應該打電話給誰來取消呢？）

實用會話

A The surprise party is all set.
（驚喜派對都準備好了。）

B Did you remember to make the reservations?
（你記得預訂桌位嗎？）

A Yes. I reserved a table for 10.
（有，我訂了一個 10 個人的桌子。）

B But there are 13 guests coming.
（可是有 13 個客人要來啊。）

Didn't you check the guest list?
（你沒查賓客名單嗎？）

A I checked it last night.
（我昨晚有查啊。）

The other three people must have been added today.
（另外 3 個人一定是今天才加上去的。）

B Well, let's try to modify the reservation.
（好吧，那試試看去更改預訂的桌位。）

I hope it isn't too late.
（我希望現在更改不會太晚。）

A **Nonsense!** It shouldn't be.
（你胡說些什麼，應該不會太晚。）

The reservation is for two weeks from now.
（我們的預訂的是 2 個星期以後。）

B You're right.
（你說得沒錯。）

I will call them in the morning.
（我明天早上會打電話給他們。）

A Maybe you should call right now.
（也許你應該現在打電話過去。）

B **Okay.** I will do that, just to be safe.
（好，保險起見，我現在就打電話。）

加強練習

➢ Nonsense!

A: Mary said she was in bed sick all day.

B: Nonsense! I saw Mary at the mall this afternoon.

A：瑪莉說她整天都生病、躺在床上。

B：你胡說些什麼，我今天下午還在大型購物中心看到她。

➢ Okay.

A: I am finished folding the laundry.

B: Okay. Now go clean the kitchen.

A：我把洗好的衣服都摺好了。

B：好吧，現在去清理廚房吧。

單字

office [ˈɔfɪs] 辦公室

cancel [ˈkænsḷ] ⓥ 取消；中止

guest [gɛst] 客人

add [æd] 加

modify [ˈmɑdəfaɪ] 更改

nonsense [ˈnɑnsɛns] ⓝ 胡說八道

safe [sef] ⓐ保險的

laundry [ˈlɔndrɪ] 待洗或洗好的衣物

fold [fold] ⓥ 折疊

Unit

4. Book tickets for a show

（預訂表演的門票）

實用例句

- Let's get tickets to see the Mavericks game!
（我們買票去看小牛隊的比賽吧。）

- Hannah can book our tickets for the show at a 10% discount.
（漢娜可以幫我們訂那場秀的票，並打 9 折。）

- Will you check to see if anyone has booked our tickets to see Romeo and Juliet?
（請你幫我看看，是否有人幫我們訂了「羅密歐與茱麗葉」的票？）

- I am going to reserve opera tickets for my parents.
（我要去幫我父母訂歌劇的票。）

- Who can book tickets for the basketball game?
（誰可以去訂籃球比賽的票？）

實用會話

A I called the local radio station to try and win tickets to the hockey game, but I didn't win.

（我打電話去本地的廣播電臺，嘗試要贏得冰上曲棍球的門票，但沒贏。）

B I have tickets to Friday's game.

（我有星期五比賽的門票。）

A **No way!** How did you get those?

（不可能吧，你怎麼拿到票的？）

B I won them in a raffle at my job.

（從公司摸彩遊戲中贏來的。）

I have two tickets.

（我有 2 張票。）

Would you like to go with me?

（要和我一起去嗎？）

A **Dang!** I would go, but I have to work on Friday.

（可惡，如果不是星期五要工作的話，我就會去。）

B Well, if you are able to take off, let me know.

（如果你可以請假的話，再告訴我吧。）

My offer still stands.

（我的邀請仍然有效。）

A Thanks. I will keep you posted.

（謝謝，我會和你保持聯絡的。）

B What day were you trying to go?

（你本來哪一天想去看？）

A The radio station had tickets for Saturday's game.

（廣播電台的票是星期六的比賽。）

B Perhaps I can trade mine in for Saturday.

（也許我可以把我的票換成星期六的。）

I will let you know.

（再通知你吧。）

加強練習

➢ No way!

A: I won the lottery today.

B: No way! I have been playing for years and never win.

A：我今天贏得樂透了。

B：不可能吧，我玩了好幾年也從來沒贏過。

➢ Dang!

A: Dang! I spilled milk on the floor.

B: I will get you a towel to wipe it up.

A：可惡，我把牛奶濺到地上了。

B：我幫你拿紙巾來擦吧。

單字

discount [ˈdɪskaʊnt] 折扣

opera [ˈɑpərə] 歌劇

win [wɪn] 贏

hockey [ˈhɑkɪ] 曲棍球

station [ˈsteʃən] 電（視）台

offer [ˈɔfɚ] ⓝ 提出；提供

post [post] 向 … 提供最新消息

trade [tred] 交換

perhaps [pɚˈhæps] 或許

spill [spɪl] 打翻（飲料）；濺出

milk [mɪlk] 牛奶

wipe [waɪp] 擦拭

Unit 5. Make an appointment
（約時間見面）

實用例句

- You should schedule an appointment with Dr. Glass.
（你應該和葛斯醫生約個時間。）

- I need to call the receptionist and schedule an interview for next week.
（我應該打電話給接待員，排個時間下星期面試。）

- I need the number for the clinic to make an appointment.
（我需要診所的電話，以便約個時間去看診。）

- Did you remember to make an appointment with your dentist?
（你是否記得和你的牙醫師約時間？）

- Ted selected an interview time for the open position.
（泰德為了那個空的職缺，安排了一個面試時間。）

實用會話

A I haven't been feeling well lately.
（我最近覺得不太舒服。）

B **Oh, really?**
（真的嗎？）

Maybe you should see a doctor.
（也許你該去看醫生。）

A I hate going to the doctor.
（我討厭看醫生。）

I end up going in and waiting for hours.
（我上次看醫生，等了好幾個小時。）

B Do you make an appointment?
（你有約好時間嗎？）

A No, I just walk in and get on the waiting list.
（沒有，我只是走進去，排進了等候名單。）

B Try making an appointment in advance.
（試著事先約好時間。）

It usually takes less time that way.
（通常事先預約都會快一點。）

A **Okay.**
（好的。）

I will call and make an appointment for tomorrow.
（我會先打電話，預約明天。）

B You should go as soon as possible.
（你越快去越好。）

A I am sure all of the appointments are booked for today.
（我確定今天的預約都滿了。）

B Okay. Make sure you call the doctor today.
（好，你今天一定要打電話給醫生。）

加強練習

➢ Oh, really?

A: I have a confession to make.
B: Oh, really? Let's hear it.

A：我想懺悔。
B：真的？說說看吧。

➢ Okay.

A: Okay. Do you prefer the pink dress or the white dress?
B: I like the pink one better.

A：好的，妳比較喜歡粉紅色還是白色洋裝？

B：我比較喜歡粉紅色的。

單字

schedule ['skɛdʒʊl] ⓥ 安排（時間）

appointment [ə'pɔɪntmənt] 約會；約定時間

receptionist [rɪ'sɛpʃənɪst] 接待員

interview ['ɪntɚvju] ⓝ 面談

clinic ['klɪnɪk] 診所

dentist ['dɛntɪst] 牙醫

select [sə'lɛkt] 選擇

position [pə'zɪʃən] ⓝ 職位

lately ['letlɪ] 近來；最近的

usually ['juʒʊəlɪ] (adv) 通常

possible ['pɑsəbḷ] ⓐ可能的

confession [kən'fɛʃən] 懺悔

prefer [prɪ'fɝ] 較喜歡

COMPLAINING

抱怨

Unit 1. At work
（工作上）

實用例句

- I never get enough vacation days at this job.
（在這份工作上，我從沒有得到充分的假期。）

- Suzy hates her job.
（蘇茜討厭她的工作。）

- My job is quite boring.
（我的工作相當無聊。）

- Every time I see Andy, he's complaining about the empty coffee pot.
（每次我看到安迪，他都在抱怨咖啡壺是空的。）

- I have piles of paperwork to clear at work.
（我辦公室有一疊疊的文件要處理。）

實用會話

A I am so tired of staring at the ever-growing

piles on my desk at the office!
（我厭倦了看著辦公室桌上一直不斷累積的文件。）

B **Tell me about it!** My desk is covered in paperwork, too.
（這還用你說，我的桌子也被文件蓋住了。）

A Every day the boss gives me a new project before I complete the other ones.
（每天在我處理完舊的文件前，我老闆就會給我新的。）

B Why are bosses so inconsiderate?
（為什麼老闆都不會為員工著想？）

A I don't know.
（我不知道。）

I am fed up with that place.
（我受夠了那個地方。）

I may be looking for a new job soon.
（也許很快就得找份新工作。）

B I can't leave my job.
（我不能離開我的工作。）

They have good medical benefits, so I am stuck there.
（他們提供好的醫療保障，所以我走不掉。）

A I have been there for three years, and I have

never been given a raise!

（我在那邊也工作 3 年了，從來沒加過薪。）

B **Gosh!** You should go to your supervisor and request a pay increase.

（哇，那你應該去找你的上司，要求加薪。）

A I have tried.

（我試過了。）

B Well, it probably *is* time for you to look for a new job.

（也許找新工作的時機到了。）

加強練習

➢ Tell me about it!

A: The more I try to save money, the more bills I have to pay.

B: Tell me about it! I am up to my ears in unpaid bills.

A：我越是想省錢，就有越多的帳單要付。

B：這還用你說，我都快被未付帳單給淹沒了呢。

➢ Gosh!

A: Can you be quiet?

B: Gosh! I was already whispering.

A：你可以安靜一點嗎？

B：哇，我已經是用耳語低聲交談了。

單字

hate [het] 恨；不喜歡

boring ['borɪŋ] 乏味的

quite [kwaɪt] 非常

empty ['ɛmptɪ] 空的；用罄

pot [pɑt] 壺

complain [kəm'plen] ⓥ 抱怨；控訴

pile [paɪl] 一疊

complete [kəm'plit] 完成

boss [bɔs] ⓝ 主管；老闆

inconsiderate [ɪnkən'sɪdərɪt] 不體貼的

stuck [stʌk] 困住

benefit ['bɛnəfɪt] ⓝ 福利

raise [rez] 加薪

request [rɪ'kwɛst] 要求

increase [ɪn'kris] 增加；增強

whisper ['hwɪspɚ] 輕聲細語

Unit

2. The traffic is awful.

（交通真是糟透了）

實用例句

- I was in traffic for an hour on my way home from work.
（從公司回家的路上，我花了一個小時通車。）

- I am going to wait a while before I leave to avoid the awful traffic.
（我想等一下再離開，以避免糟糕的路況。）

- I normally ride the train so that I don't have to drive in all of the traffic.
（我通常都搭火車，所以不會遇到塞車情況。）

- There was an accident, and now traffic is backed up for miles.
（發生車禍，車陣已經回堵幾英哩了。）

- The traffic is always horrible during rush hour.
（尖峰時間的交通總是很糟。）

實用會話

A I was stuck in traffic all morning.

（我今天整個早上都被堵在車陣裡。）

B **How awful.**

（那真是太糟了。）

Were you able to get to your meeting on time?

（你有準時參加會議嗎？）

A No. I was 15 minutes late.

（沒有，我遲到了 15 分鐘。）

B Did they get upset with you for being late?

（他們有因此而生氣嗎？）

A No. I arrived first.

（不會，我還是第一個到的。）

Everyone else was also stuck in traffic.

（其他人也都塞在車陣裡。）

B Well, that worked out better than I expected.

（那情況比我預期的好。）

A **Exactly**. There was a bad accident that caused traffic to pile up.

（一點也沒錯，發生了嚴重的車禍，造成交通回堵。）

B Was anyone injured?

（有人受傷嗎？）

A No. Three cars were totally destroyed, but everyone was okay.
（沒有，三台車完全毀了，但每個人都還好。）

B That's good.
（那還不錯。）

Give me an update on the meeting later.
（等一下把會議的細節告訴我。）

加強練習

➢ How awful.

A: My pet kitten died.

B: How awful. Is there anything I can do?

A：我的寵物小貓咪死了。

B：真是太糟了，有什麼事我可以幫忙的嗎？

➢ Exactly.

A: We should have a Hawaiian theme for our next party.

B: Exactly. I was thinking the same thing.

A：我們下次的舞會應該以夏威夷為主題。

B：一點也沒錯，我也有同樣的想法。

單字

traffic ['træfɪk] 交通

awful ['ɔfʊl] ⓐ 很糟的；可怕的

normally ['nɔrməlɪ] 通常；一般來說

horrible ['hɔrəbḷ] （口語）糟透的；可怕的

upset ['ʌp'sɛt] 不高興

expect [ɪk'spɛkt] 預期；期待

injure ['ɪndʒɚ] 受傷

destroy ['dɪstrɔɪ] 毀壞

update ['ʌp'det] 更新

theme [θim] 主題

Unit

3. The service is terrible

（服務真是糟透了）

實用例句

- Never eat at Pappasito's restaurant. The service is terrible.
  （絕對不要去 Pappasito 餐廳，那裡的服務很糟。）

- The waiter at this trendy restaurant spilled coffee all over me.
  （這家時髦餐廳的侍者，把咖啡濺在我身上了。）

- I received the wrong order when I went to the coffeehouse last night.
  （我昨晚去咖啡廳時，他們把我點的菜弄錯了。）

- It is so hard to find good service these days!
  （近來要找到好服務是件難事。）

- Jenny told me never to eat at Denny's because of the poor service.
  （珍妮告訴我別去丹尼餐廳用餐，因為他們的服務不好。）

實用會話

A Judy and James hate eating at Denny's.
（茱蒂和詹姆士討厭去丹尼餐廳吃東西。）

B **Really?** The food is great.
（真的嗎？那裡的食物不錯啊。）

A Yes, but the service is terrible.
（是的，但服務真的很糟。）

B They had to wait 35 minutes to be seated.
（他們等了 35 分鐘才被帶位。）

A That's not so bad.
（這樣還不算很糟。）

Denny's can be crowded.
（丹尼餐廳生意有時很好。）

B There were plenty of tables.
（當時還有很多座位。）

They were understaffed and couldn't handle another table, so they made customers wait.
（該餐廳人手不足，不能多照顧其他桌，所以就讓讓顧客們等候。）

A **That's unfair.**
（這是不公平的。）

I would have left immediately.
（要是我，我會立刻離開。）

B Judy and James decided to stay, hoping the dinner would be worth the wait.
（茱蒂和詹姆士決定留下，希望好吃的晚餐值的他們等待。）

A How was the food?
（食物如何？）

B The food was cold and undercooked.
（食物是冷的，而且沒煮熟。）

加強練習

➤ Really?

A: I can meet you next Tuesday for lunch.
B: Really? That sounds great.

A：我可以下星期二跟你吃午餐。
B：真的嗎？那太好了。

➤ That's unfair.

A: I don't like John.
B: That's unfair. You don't even know him.

A：我不喜歡約翰。
B：這不公平，你甚至還不認識他。

單字

restaurant [ˈrɛstərənt] ⓝ餐館；飯店

service [ˈsɝvɪs] 服務

terrible [ˈtɛrəbl̩] 差勁的；（口語）糟透的；可怕的

trendy [ˈtrɛndɪ] 時髦的

crowded [ˈkraʊdɪd] ⓐ 擁擠的

customer [ˈkʌstəmɚ] ⓝ 顧客

understaffed [ʌndɚˈstæft] 雇員不夠

handle [ˈhændl̩] 處理

unfair [ʌnˈfɛr] 不公平的

Unit

4. At home

（在家中）

實用例句

- All I ever do at home is clean up after everyone!
（我在家裡只做一件事，那就是清理每個人製造出來的垃圾。）

- There is never any toothpaste left in the bathroom.
（浴室從來沒剩下任何牙膏。）

- I am tired of cooking dinner and having no one eat it.
（我厭倦了準備晚餐卻沒人吃。）

- This house is a mess!
（這個家真是髒成一堆。）

- Children, go clean your filthy rooms!
（孩子們，去整理你們骯髒的房間。）

實用會話

A I hate my apartment.
（我討厭我的公寓。）

B What is wrong with it?
（怎麼了嗎？）

A It is too small and cramped.
（又小又擁擠。）

B You should move.
（你應該搬家。）

Maybe you could find a bigger one.
（也許你可以找一個更大的地方。）

A **Ha!** It's not that simple.
（嘿，這沒那麼簡單。）

I can't afford a bigger place.
（我付不起更大的公寓。）

B **I see.** Well, what else is wrong besides the small space?
（我懂了，除了太小，那地方還有什麼不好嗎？）

A The carpet is dingy and stained.
（地毯很髒，而且有污點）

B That sounds unpleasant.
（聽起來真令人感到不舒服。）

A It is. I have to deal with it for now.

（就是啊，我現在得忍受這情況。）

B Things will get better when you make a little more money and can move to a better place.

（當你賺多一點錢，就可以搬到比較好的地方，情況就會好多了。）

加強練習

➢ Ha!

A: Can I borrow $1,000?

B: Ha! Do I look like I am made of money?

A：我可以跟你借 1000 元嗎？

B：嘿，我看起來像是個金庫嗎？

➢ I see.

A: I am going to play basketball.

B: I see. Well, have a nice workout.

A：我要去打籃球。

B：我知道了，好好玩。

單字

toothpaste [ˈtuθpæst] 牙膏

mess [mɛs] 亂七八糟；一團糟

filthy [ˈfɪlθɪ] 骯髒的

cramped [kræmpt] 峽窄的

besides [bɪˈsaɪdz] prep. 除了……之外

stained [stend] 沾污的

dingy [ˈdɪŋgɪ] 褪色的

unpleasant [ʌnˈplɛzn̩t] 不愉快的

Unit 5. At the hotel
（旅館）

實用例句

- This hotel has dirty bathrooms.
  （這間旅館的浴室很髒。）

- Our hotel room had no clean towels.
  （我們旅館房間內，沒有乾淨的毛巾）

- Our maid never came to clean up our hotel room.
  （我們的女服務生從不來打掃旅館房間。）

- Our luggage was stolen from our hotel suite.
  （我們的行李從旅館套房中被偷走了。）

- The desk clerk was very rude to us at check-in.
  （當我們報到時，櫃檯人員對我們很沒禮貌。）

實用會話

A Has the maid come to clean our hotel room?

（女服務生把我們的房間整理好了嗎？）

B Not yet. Perhaps she will come later on.
（還沒，也許她等一下會來。）

A **My goodness!**
（天啊。）

It is already past noon!
（都已經過了中午了。）

B **That's true.**
（這倒是真的。）

She should have come by now.
（她早就應該過來了。）

A I am tired of the bad service at this hotel.
（我受夠了這家旅館的爛服務。）

The food I ordered through room service was cold.
（我客房服務點來的餐居然是冷的。）

B I slipped on a wet floor in the lobby.
（我還在大廳的溼地板上滑倒呢！）

A We should file a formal complaint about these incidents.
（我們應該針對這些事件，提出正式抱怨。）

B Yeah. You're right.

（對，你說的對。）

A We shouldn't have to accept this bad service.

（我們不應該被迫接受這樣的爛服務。）

B I know.

（我知道。）

We pay too much for *this* kind of treatment.

（這樣的招待太浪費我們的錢了。）

加強練習

➢ My goodness!

A: My goodness! You startled me.

B: Sorry. I didn't mean to. I thought you saw me standing here.

A：天啊，你嚇了我一跳。

B：抱歉，我不是故意的，我以為你看到我站在這邊。

➢ That's true.

A: Mandy is such a talented singer.

B: That's true. She has a great voice.

A：曼蒂是個有天份的歌星。

B：這倒是真的，她的歌聲很美。

單字

dirty [ˈdɝtɪ] 髒的

towel [ˈtaʊəl] 毛巾

never [ˈnɛvɚ] 從未；未曾

luggage [ˈlʌgɪdʒ] 行李

rude [rud] 無禮的；魯莽的

maid [med] 女傭；清潔女工

past [pæst] 超越

slip [slɪp] 滑

lobby [ˈlɑbɪ] 大廳

complaint [kəmˈplent] ⓝ 埋怨；牢騷；訴苦

formal [ˈfɔrml̩] ⓐ 正式的

file [faɪl] 提出申請

treatment [ˈtritmənt] 處理

startle [ˈstɑrtl̩] 嚇著

talented [ˈtæləntɪd] ⓐ 有才藝的

10分鐘會話速成課---1億人都在用的英語書

英語系列：43

作者／張瑪麗
出版者／哈福企業有限公司
地址／新北市板橋區五權街16號
電話／(02) 2945-6285　傳真／(02) 2945-6986
郵政劃撥／31598840　戶名／哈福企業有限公司
出版日期／2017年11月
定價／NT$ 299元 (附MP3)

全球華文國際市場總代理／采舍國際有限公司
地址／新北市中和區中山路2段366巷10號3樓
電話／(02) 8245-8786　傳真／(02) 8245-8718
網址／www.silkbook.com 新絲路華文網

香港澳門總經銷／和平圖書有限公司
地址／香港柴灣嘉業街12號百樂門大廈17樓
電話／(852) 2804-6687　傳真／(852) 2804-6409
定價／港幣100元 (附MP3)

圖片／shuttlestock
email／haanet68@Gmail.com
網址／Haa-net.com
facebook／Haa-net 哈福網路商城

國家圖書館出版品預行編目資料

10分鐘會話速成課 / 張瑪麗著. -- 新北市：哈福企業, 2017.11
　面；　公分. -- (英語系列；43)
ISBN 978-986-94966-5-0(平裝附光碟片)

1.英語 2.詞彙 3.會話

805.12　　106020255

哈福

哈福

哈福